Samuel I. Prime

Thoughts on the Death of Little Children

Samuel I. Prime

Thoughts on the Death of Little Children

ISBN/EAN: 9783337404871

Printed in Europe, USA, Canada, Australia, Japan

Cover: Foto ©Andreas Hilbeck / pixelio.de

More available books at **www.hansebooks.com**

THOUGHTS

ON THE

DEATH OF LITTLE CHILDREN.

BY SAMUEL IRENÆUS PRIME, D.D.

WITH AN APPENDIX SELECTED FROM VARIOUS AUTHORS.

NEW AND ENLARGED EDITION.

NEW-YORK:

ANSON D. F. RANDOLPH,

770 BROADWAY, CORNER· OF NINTH STREET.

——

1865.

CONTENTS.

iv

Hymns and Poems.

Death of Little Children.

𝕯eath of 𝕷ittle 𝕮hildren.

CHAPTER I.

𝕿he 𝕮hild is 𝕯ead.

IT is hard to believe it: that we shall no
more hear the glad voice, nor meet the merry
laugh that burst so often from its glad heart.

Child as it was, it was a pleasant child, and
to the partial parent there are traits of love-
liness that no other eye may see. It was a
wise ordering of Providence that we should
love our own children as no one else loves
them, and as we love the children of none
besides. And ours was a lovely child.

But the child is dead. You may put away
its playthings. Put them where they will be
safe. I would not like to have them broken
or lost; and you need not lend them to other
children when they come to see us. It would

pain me to see them in other hands, much as I love to see children happy with their toys.

Its clothes you may lay aside; I shall often look them over, and each of the colors that he wore will remind me of him as he looked when he was here. I shall weep often when I think of him;. but there is a luxury in thinking of the one that is gone, which I would not part with for the world. I think of my child now, a child always, though an angel among angels.

The child is dead. The eye has lost its lustre. The hand is still and cold. Its little heart is not beating now. How pale it looks! Yet the very form is dear to me. Every lock of its hair, every feature of the face, is a treasure that I shall prize the more, as the months of my sorrow come and go.

Lay the little one in his coffin. He was never in so cold and hard a bed, but he will feel it not. He would not know it, if he had been laid in his cradle, or in his mother's arms. Throw a flower or two by his side: like them he withered.

Carry him out to the grave. Gently. It is a hard road this to the grave. Every jar seems to disturb the infant sleeper. Here we are, at the brink of the sepulchre. Oh, how damp, and dark, and cold! But the dead do not feel it. There is no pain, no fear, no weeping there. Sleep on now, and take your rest!

Fill it up! Ashes to ashes, dust to dust! Every clod seems to fall on my heart. Every smothered sound from the grave is saying, Gone, gone, gone! It is full now. Lay the turf gently over the dear child. Plant a myrtle among the sods, and let the little one sleep among the trees and flowers. Our child is not there. His dust, precious dust, indeed, is there, but our child is in heaven. He is not here; he is risen.

I shall think of the form that is mouldering here among the dead; and it will be a mournful comfort to come at times, and think of the child that was once the light of our house, and the idol—ah! that I must own the secret of this sorrow—the idol of my heart.

And it is beyond all language to express the joy, in the midst of tears, I feel, that my sin, in making an idol of the child, has not made that infant less dear to Jesus. Nay, there is even something that tells me the Saviour called the darling from me, that I might love the Saviour more when I had one child less to love. He knoweth our frame;

he knows the way to win and bind us. **Dear Saviour**, as thou hast my lamb, give *me* too a place in thy bosom. Set me as a seal on thy heart.

And now let us go back to the house. It is strangely changed. It is silent and cheerless, gloomy even. When did I enter this door without the greeting of those lips and eyes, that I shall greet no more? Can the absence of but one produce so great a change so soon? When one of the children was away on a visit, we did not feel the absence as we do now. That was for a time; this is for ever. He will not return. Hark! I thought for a moment it was the child, but it was only my own heart's yearning for the lost. He will not come again.

*   *   *   *

Such thoughts as these have been the thoughts of many in the season of their first grief.

As heart answereth to the heart, there is a wondrous likeness in the sorrow of parents over the death of their little ones. The rich and the poor, the learned and the ignorant are alike, when they sit by the side of their babes in the struggles of death; and when they follow them to the grave, their hearts are true to nature, and nature mourns when the loved are torn away.

One of the iron sort of men, a man of war, sent for me to come and see him in his affliction. His child, a sweet girl of three or four years only, had been taken with the croup, and died before medical relief could be obtained. He met me in his hall, and fell on my neck, and wept like a child. I had never seen him weep before. I had never thought that such a man as he had tears to shed. And I do not know that he would have wept, had the pestilence or the sword swept off all the rest of those whom he loved, and spared the infant that nestled in his bosom.

If this is a weakness to those who have never tasted the cup, I am sure that none of them will be offended with these words, for they will not read them till they are weeping too. To be a brother in sorrow, you must have suffered. Even the Lord of heaven had to become a man, that he might, by his experience, learn to bear our sorrows. And then he wept with those who wept.

Some time ago I was at the funeral of the child of a pastor; and when the neighboring minister, who had been called upon to bury his brother's child, had closed his words of sympathy and comfort, the stricken father rose and said: "When I have sought to minister to your consolation in the times of your affliction, weeping with you over your dying children, you have often said to me that I knew nothing of the anguish, and could not sympathize with you in your loss. I feel it now. I never did before." And then he pointed them to the sources of comfort that God was opening to his soul, and asked them to come to the fountain and drink. The house in which we were then assembled stood on a hill-side, overlooking a beautiful river, and, on the other side of it, "sweet fields stood drest in living green." The pastor went on to say—and there was a strange power and beauty, too, in the words as they fell from his lips in the midst of tears—"Often, as I have stood on the borders of this stream, and looked over to the fair fields on the other shore, I have felt but little interest in the people or the place in full view before me. The river separates me from them, and my thoughts and affections were here. But a few months ago, one of my children moved across to the other side, and took up his residence there. Since that time, my heart has been there also. In the morning, when I rise and look out toward the east, I think of my child who is over there, and again and again through the day I think of him, and the other side of the river is always in my thoughts with the child who is gone there to dwell. And now, since another of my children has crossed the river of death, and has gone to dwell on the other side, my heart is drawn out toward heaven and the inhabitants of heaven as it was never drawn before. I supposed that heaven was dear to me; that my Father was there, and my friends were there, and that I had a great interest in heaven, but I *had no child there!* Now I have; and I never think and never shall think of heaven, but with the memory of that dear child who is to be among its inhabitants for ever."

It was a beautiful and impressive illustration. The heart of the father was soothed by thoughts like these. He loved to look away to heaven, and think of it as the abode of his child, a seraph now, happier far than he could be in this vale of tears, and happier than he would ever have been, had he lived to grow up to manhood, to die in sin.

The Rev. Dr. Pye was called to part with

two children, a son and a daughter. A few days afterwards, he wrote a letter as if it had come from the girl just after she had ceased to breathe, and a little before her brother's death. Here is an extract from the letter which he supposes his child to write:

"It was he who made us that called us away, and we cheerfully obeyed the summons; and I must now tell you, though you already know it, that he expects from you not only that you meekly and calmly submit to such a seemingly severe dispensation of his providence, but that you also rejoice with me in it, because it is the will and pleasure of our divine Father. I, young as I was, am now an inhabitant of heaven, and already see the beauty and harmony of that little chain of events which related to my short abode in your world, and even the manner of my leaving it; and when you see the things as they really are, and not as they now appear, you will confess and adore the divine goodness, even in taking us so soon from your embraces.

"Ask not why it has pleased God so early to remove us; we sufficiently answered the great end of our being if, while living, at the same time that we gave you pleasure, you

were disposed to lead us, by your examples
and precepts, into the paths of virtue and religion ; and if now, by the loss of us, you become examples of patience and submission to
the divine will.

"Let, therefore, all the little incidents in
our past lives, the remembrance of which is
too apt to renew your sorrow, be so many oc-
casions of your joy, inasmuch as they may
recall the pleasant ideas you once delighted
in ; and let the dismaying and melancholy
remembrance of our sickness and early death
be changed into cheering and bright ideas of
what we now enjoy, and what you, I hope,
will one day see us in possession of."

There was something very comforting in
this thought, of the child departed sending
back a message to the mourning parent. I
doubt not that children in heaven are aston-
ished, if they know that their parents here,
on the earth, are grieving on their account.
"If our parents only knew what we have
gained, how soon they would dry their
tears !"

The lady of Sir Stamford Raffles, in India,
was overwhelmed with grief for the loss of a
favorite child, unable to bear the sight of her
other children, unable to bear even the light

of day. She was lying upon her couch, with a feeling of desolation that was fast growing into despair, when she was addressed by a poor, ignorant woman, one of the natives, who had been employed in the nursery: "I am come," said the servant, "because you have been here many days shut up in a dark room, and no one dares to come near you. Are you not ashamed to grieve in this manner, when you ought to be thanking God for having given you the most beautiful child that ever was seen? Did any one ever see him or speak of him without admiring him? And, instead of letting this child continue in this world till he should be worn out with trouble and sorrow, has not God taken him to heaven in all his beauty? What would you have more? For shame! leave off weeping, and let me open a window."

It is not always wise to bid a mourner "leave off weeping." Tears are sometimes good for the soul. That grief is very bitter which cannot find tears. I have often wished that they would come, and relieve this dry and dreadful pressure on the heart. But if we do not cease to weep, by all means let us open the window. Let us have the light of God's countenance shining upon us like the sun at noon. To shut ourselves up in the dark to brood over our sorrows, is the worst of all remedies for grief. To cherish our afflictions, as if they were to be indulged, and petted, and kept fresh as long as possible, and as if it were wrong for us to go out into the world, and mingle in the duties and pleasures of social Christian life, is a sinful yielding to the power of a dispensation that was not designed to be thus received.

The pious Flavel says- -and there is great wisdom in these words of his—"Mourner, whatever may be your grief for the death of your children, it might have been still greater for their life. Bitter experience once led a good man to say, 'It is better to weep for ten children dead, than for one living.' Remember the heart-piercing affliction of David, whose son sought his life. Your love for your children will hardly admit of the thought of such a thing as possible in your own case. They appeared innocent and amiable; and you fondly believed that, through your care and prayers, they would have become the joy of your hearts. But parents much more frequently see the vices of their children than their virtues. And even should your children prove amiable and promising, you might

live to be the wretched witness of their sufferings. Some parents have felt unutterable
agonies of this kind. God may have taken
the lamented objects of your affection from
the evil to come."

A mother, suddenly convinced that her
child was dying, sent for a man of God to
come and pray for the child's life. "Shall I
not pray," said he, "that the will of the Lord
may be done, and that you may have strength
to suffer all that holy will?" "No," she
answered in the agony of her heart, "no, no!
I want my child to live. Pray for his life, or
do not pray at all." The child lived, and
lived to be a man, a great man; but oh, how
wicked! and to pierce that mother's heart
with pangs of anguish which made that night
almost a night of joy, when she would not
let her infant die. We do not know from
what our infants are saved, when they are
saved from draining the cup of life.

"In another life," says Fenelon, "we shall
see and understand the wonders of His goodness that have escaped us in this; and we
shall rejoice at what has made us weep on
earth. Alas! in our present darkness, we
cannot see either our true good or evil. If
God were to gratify our desires, it would be

our ruin. He saves us by breaking the ties that bind us to earth. We complain because God loves us better than we know how to love ourselves. We weep because he has taken those whom we love away from temptation and sin. God takes the poisonous cup from our hands, and we weep as a child weeps when its mother takes away the shining weapon with which it would pierce its own breast.

"Oh! consider, ere you accuse Providence for the stroke, that this death, apparently so untimely, is possibly the greatest instance toward you both of the mercy and love of God. The creature so dear to you may have been taken from some sad reverse of fortune, or from the commission of some great crime, which might have endangered his salvation. To secure this, God has removed him from temptation. The pang of separation is indeed most bitter, yet our merciful Father does not needlessly afflict his creatures. He wounds only to heal the diseases of our souls. Let us, then, in the hour of our calamity, hold fast by this conviction, and say with Job, ' Though he slay me, yet will I trust in him.' His mercy can be my support here, and my recompense hereafter."

This is the spirit of Christian submission to the will of Heaven. With such a spirit is the grace that says, "Even so, Father, for so it seemeth good in thy sight." And this same holy Fenelon was called to the trial of his faith. Standing by the coffin of one whom he most tenderly loved, and for whom he would most cheerfully have died a thousand deaths, he cried:

"There he lies, and all my worldly happiness lies dead with him. But if the turning of a straw would call him back to life, I would not for ten thousand worlds be the turner of that straw, in opposition to the will of God."

"I have had six children," said Mr. Eliot, " and I bless God for his free grace, they are all with Christ, or in Christ; and my mind is now at rest concerning them. My desire was that they should have served Christ on earth; but if God will choose to have them serve him in heaven, I have nothing to object to it. His will be done."

Yes, I will say so likewise: His will be done. It is the best and wisest will; and though it does darken all my prospects, and disappoint a thousand cherished hopes, I know that he who has done it doeth all things well. I can trust him for this, as I have never trusted him yet, when his promises have failed.

"I sincerely sympathize with you," says Dr. Erskine, to a friend who had lost an only son, "in your heavy trial. I have drunk deep of the same cup; of *nine sons*, only one survives. From what I repeatedly felt, I can form an idea what you must feel. I cannot, I dare not say, weep not. Jesus wept at the grave of Lazarus, and surely he allows you to weep. But oh, let hope and joy mitigate your heaviness. I know not how this shall work for your good; but it is enough that God knows. He that said, 'All things shall work together for good to them that love God,' excepts not from this promise the sorest trial. You devoted your son to God; you cannot doubt that he accepted the surrender. If he has been hid in the chamber of the grave from the evil of sin and from the evil of suffering, let not your eye be evil, when God is good. What you chiefly wished for him, and prayed on his behalf, was spiritual and heavenly blessings. If the greatest thing you wished for is accomplished, at the season and in the manner Infinite Wisdom saw best, refuse not to be comforted. You know not what work and what joy have been waiting for him in that other world."

An old tomb-stone bears this epitaph, and one might think an angel whispers it to a mourning mother's ear:

> " Weep not, my mother, weep not; I am blest,
>   But must leave heaven, if I *come to thee;*
> For I am where the weary are at rest,
>   The wicked cease from troubling. *Come to me.*"

   *   *   *   *

I know there are thousands of hearts that will read these chapters, not with sympathy only, but with comfort and sacred peace. There is scarcely a house in the world, into which the sorrow has not come which follows the death of a child. It is almost literally true—

> "There is no flock, however watched and tended,
>   But one dead lamb is there;
> There is no fireside, howsoe'er defended,
>   But has one vacant chair."

The child is dead. Our child is dead. Let us now go to the book of God, and learn its lessons in the time of our affliction.

CHAPTER II.

Can I bring him back again?

THE child of David, the bard and king, was dead. His son, his favorite son, his precious, well-beloved, best-beloved son, was dead. For seven long, anxious days and nights, while the scale trembled in suspense, he had fasted and wept. Kings' children die:

> "———Death, with impartial fate,
> Knocks at the palace door and cottage gate."

The crown often rests on an aching head, and the royal purple covers a sad heart, when the messenger of the grave steals into the king's chamber, and stops the breath of his babes. It is so in ours.

The kind attendants of the stricken father reasoned wisely, as they reason who do not understand the power of true religion. They said among themselves: He was weeping and praying while the child was yet alive; how he will vex himself, how much greater will be his anguish, now the child is dead! They mistook the man. They judged him by their own standard, and were wrong. The pious father drew from a deeper fountain, and found waters they knew not of. He reasoned on other principles than those which lie on the surface of things, and he was strengthened.

He saw the servants whispering, and thought it was probably all over with the child. It was a sign that death was in the house, when even the servants would not speak above their breath. The dead cannot hear, but the living are still when death is at hand.

And David asked, "Is the child dead?"

And they answered, "He is dead."

Then David arose from the earth, and washed and anointed himself, and changed his apparel, and *came into the house of the Lord,* AND WORSHIPPED.

Then he came to his own house, and when he required, they set bread before him, and he did eat. And the servants were filled with wonder that a father thus stricken with grief should so suddenly find comfort in his sorrow; and they said unto him,

"What thing is this that thou hast done? Thou didst fast and weep for the child while it was alive, but when the child was dead, thou didst arise and eat bread."

And David answered, "While the child was

yet alive, I fasted and wept; for I said, 'Who can tell whether God will be gracious to me, that the child may live?' But now he is dead, wherefore should I fast? Can I bring him back again? I shall go to him, but he shall not return to me."

"*Can I bring him back again?*" A sad inquiry. *Can* I bring him back again? Not *Would* I? Perhaps he would. Perhaps we would. But CAN I? Had tears availed to save, the child would not have died. Had prayer prevailed, the boy would yet be living, the joy of his parents' hearts, and the light of their eyes. But he is dead. He is gone. Could human skill avert the death-blow, he would have been saved. But all was done that skill could do, and yet he died. And there he lies. Can I bring him to life again? I may weep, but my tears fall on his icy brow, and he feels them not. His heart is still. He breathes no more. The love and wit of men are alike in vain to restore the spirit of this lifeless clay. Speak to it, and it hears not. Kiss it, and its lips are cold. Press it to your bosom, and it is not warmed. The child is dead, dead; and can I bring it back again? Ah, if I could! If rivers of waters running down my eyes, if oceans of tears would float his spirit back to this deserted shell that once was animated with his precious soul, I would weep day and night for my departed.

But it is fruitless. And it is not the part of a rational being to expend the energies of his nature on that which avails him nothing. This may be the least and lowest source of comfort that reason offers to a mind distressed, but it is the dictate of wisdom, and grace adds its sanctions to the conclusion forced upon us by the law of nature. It is the will of God, and we cannot change the purpose if we would.

We cannot bring him back again. *Then* and *therefore* let us lay his ashes in their kindred dust, close the green turf over his mouldering form, and turn to the book of God for consolation in the day of our calamity.

CHAPTER III.

He is not lost, though gone.

It is clearly revealed that God employs the spirits whom he has made, to minister unto those whom he delights to tend with peculiar care. With the mode of angelic or spiritual intercourse, we are not acquainted. That disembodied spirits, the evil and the good, are permitted to reach our minds and exert a power on our spirits, is not to be doubted, though we may be unable to respond to that influence, and, at the moment of its communication, may be unconscious of its presence.

"Millions of spiritual beings walk the earth unseen, both when we wake and when we sleep." And we believe, with many others, that if we were suddenly divested of this mortal, we should find ourselves in a vast amphitheatre, reaching to the throne of God, filled with spirits, the unseen witnesses, the clouds of witnesses with whom we are encompassed continually. There is a place where the Most High dwells in light that no man can approach, where the darkness of excessive brightness hangs over and around His throne, making *Heaven,* as Heaven is not elsewhere in the universe of God. But neither time nor place may with propriety be affirmed of spiritual existence. When Gabriel leaves his throne to execute the high behests of the Almighty, there is no intervening time or space between his departure and his presence, where his work is to be done. We use the terms that are adapted to our mode of existence, and are lost when we attempt to express the life of those whose nature is in another scale and order of beings than our own. It is, therefore, scriptural and rational to suppose that the spirits of our departed friends are around us by day and night; not away from God: his presence fills immensity; he is every where present. If an angel or the soul of a saint should take the wings of the morning, and dwell in the uttermost part of the sea, there to be with us or with those we love, even there the gracious presence of God would dwell, and the sanctified would find *Heaven* as blessed and glorious as in the temple of which the Lamb is the light.

We must be near to one another, to see and be seen, to hear and be heard. Our bodily organs are of necessity restricted, and hence

we have the impression that spirits must be
bound by the same fetters.   But this is an
illusion that vanishes, when we reflect that
speech, and sound, and sight, are attributes
belonging to spirits only to accommodate us
in our conception of communication with
them.   *Thought* is the language of the soul.
Words are needed to convey that thought
through the organs of the body to another
soul.   If there were no intervening body, I
know not that the soul has any need of words.
Sympathy is doubtless felt through all the
spiritual world, without those channels of
intelligence that we must open and explore.
There is joy among the angels when a sinner
repents, or a saint expires, long before the
news is whispered from throne to throne,
through the palaces of the skies.   The thrill
is more than electric.   It is instant and every
where in the empire of holy mind.

If, then, there is such conscious sympathy
among the spirits of the blest, who will deny
that they, whose angels do always behold the
face of the Father, are also conversant with
those whom they have left on earth?   The
dead are with us and around us, and, though
gone, are not lost.   Wherever, in the world
of spirits, God may have fixed the habitation

of his throne, it is right to believe that his essential presence is every where, and his saints are where they can be the happiest, and best perform his high and holy will.

All this proceeds upon the doctrine, that the souls of infants do immediately pass into glory, when released from the prison of the flesh. This truth is too plainly taught in the Holy Scriptures, and is too firmly rooted in the human heart, to be doubted. "Of such is the kingdom of heaven," was said by Him who said, "Suffer the little children to come unto me." The royal prophet evidently recognized this truth, when he comforted himself by the assurance that he should meet his child again. To me it has always been a delightful truth, that these little ones are, in great kindness, transplanted to a more congenial clime, and spared the ills that they must meet and buffet in a world of sin. So that I have often said, "I thank God when an infant dies." But this is gratitude felt only when the children of others die.

Yet it is a blessed thought, that when one of our children dies in infancy, it sleeps in Jesus. We are sure of one in Heaven. The rest may grow up in sin, and die in sin, and be lost, but one is safe. Thanks to God, the lost is found, the dead is alive. "The Lord gave, and the Lord hath taken away; blessed be the name of the Lord." "They only can be said to possess a child for ever, who have lost one in infancy."

CHAPTER IV.

Infinite Wisdom took him away.

"My thoughts are not your thoughts, neither are your ways my ways, saith the Lord." The truth of this we feel when clouds and darkness hang around the throne. And then we listen again, and the same voice adds, "For as the heavens are higher than the earth, so are my ways higher than your ways, and my thoughts than your thoughts."

Nothing but infinite presumption would challenge the wisdom of the divine dercees. What is man, that he should venture to doubt that He who knows all things from the beginning, before whom the future, with all its changes, is for ever present, better understands than we what is the most for his glory, and the good of his government? Could we behold the varied and benign results that, in his providence and grace, are to be the fruit of those events which we regard as painfully undesirable; could we see the glory that they will bring eventually to Him whose glory is the ultimate and righteous object of all that is, so that around the death of an infant, as around the fall of an empire, cluster consider-ations that bear upon the joys of saints, and the services of angels, and the honor of Him who sitteth in the Heavens, God over all, we would not merely acquiesce in the *dispensation*, but we should rejoice in it with joy unspeakable. It is often the severest portion of our afflictions, that we cannot see why they are sent upon us. Our faith is demanded, that we may believe where we cannot see. "What thou knowest not now, thou shalt know hereafter." "Blessed are they who have not seen, and yet have believed." That faith is grounded on our knowledge that He who orders all our ways is too wise to be mistaken. His purposes are eternal. When this earth shall have become wearied with rolling, and all the stars have fallen from their places, away in the future, millions of ages beyond the judgment of the great day, the death of a babe in the house will be working out its results in the eternal purposes of God. We may not *see* till then, perhaps not then. How far off it may be, none can tell. But it is all right, and we shall find it to be so hereafter. It requires no very *exalted* order of *faith* to adopt this sentiment, and let

the soul lie down on it confidingly, and look
up trustingly, and smile serenely, when the
hand of God presses heavily.

Oh, let my trembling soul be still,
  While darkness veils this mortal eye,
And wait thy wise, thy holy will,
  Wrapped yet in tears and mystery.
I cannot, Lord, thy purpose see,
Yet all is well, since ruled by thee.

Thus, trusting in thy love, I tread
  The narrow path of duty on.
What though some cherished joys are fled!
  What though some flattering dreams are gone!
Yet purer, brighter joys remain;
Why should my spirit then complain!

CHAPTER V.

Infinite Love called the Child.

"LIKE as a father pitieth his children, so the Lord pitieth them that fear him. For he knoweth our frame; he remembereth that we are dust."

The sovereignty of God we are bound, as his creatures, to acknowledge and adore. He has a right to do with his own what he will; and when to this we join his wisdom, it is easy to construct an argument that compels submission. So the afflicted father, whose example is our theme, was affected when he said, "I was dumb, I opened not my mouth, because thou didst it." And then he cried out, under the same emotion, "Remove thy stroke away from me: I am consumed by the blow of thy hand." This is not the highest style of Christian confidence. It is right; but it is not the sweet and joyous trust of him who rose from the earth when his child was dead, and washed, and changed his apparel, and went into the house of God and worshipped. He is not only our God, he is our

FATHER. He taught us by the lips of his Son to call him our Father; and "whom the Lord loveth, he chasteneth." "We have had fathers of our flesh who corrected us, and we gave them reverence; shall we not much rather be in subjection unto the Father of spirits, and live? For they verily for a few days chastened us after their own pleasure; but he for our profit, that we might be partakers of his holiness."

We have chastened our own children. We did it not in anger, much less in malice, or with a desire to do an injury to the one we loved. And when our Father's hand is laid on us, it is surely our duty to bear in mind that his love for his children infinitely excels our love for those who climb on our knees and hang on our necks. Oh, was it not love that gave the child; that gave us such a child; that made it lovely in our eyes, clothing it with beauty as with a garment, and shedding upon its form and spirit those gentle, winning ways that wound about our hearts, and rendered the object of our affections just the child whom we would wish to keep? We blessed God for giving. But it is the same God who hath taken away. He never changes. And *faith* assures us that it is

greater *love* that takes than gives. Was not
the lamb his own? And did he not gather it
to his own bosom? If he had not loved it,
he would not have taken it. Was it not his
own jewel? And did he not set it as a gem
in his own crown? Let the thought of murmuring be rebuked by the following beautiful story from the Mishna of the Rabbins:

"During the absence of the Rabbi Meir,
his two sons died, both of them of uncommon
beauty, and enlightened in the divine law.
His wife bore them to her chamber, and laid
them upon her bed. When Rabbi Meir
returned, his first inquiry was for his sons.
His wife reached to him a goblet; he praised
the Lord at the going out of the Sabbath,
drank, and again asked, 'Where are my sons?'
'They are not far off,' she said, placing food
before him that he might eat. He was in a
genial mood, and when he had said grace after
meat, she thus addressed him: 'Rabbi, with
thy permission, I would fain propose to thee
one question.' 'Ask it then, my love,' replied
he. 'A few days ago, a person intrusted
some jewels to my custody, and now he
demands them; should I give them back to
him?' 'This is a question,' said the Rabbi,
'which my wife should not have thought it

necessary to ask. What! wouldst thou hesitate or be reluctant to restore to every one his own?' 'No,' she replied, 'but yet I thought it best not to restore them without acquainting thee therewith.' She then led him to the chamber, and, stepping to the bed, took the white covering from the dead bodies. 'Ah! my sons, my sons,' loudly lamented their father. 'My sons! the light of my eyes, and the light of my understanding: I was your father, but you were my teachers in the law.' The mother turned away and wept bitterly. At length she took her husband by the hand and said, 'Rabbi, didst thou not teach me that we must not be reluctant to restore that which was intrusted to our keeping? See; the Lord gave, and the Lord hath taken away, and blessed be the name of the Lord.' 'Blessed be the name of the Lord,' echoed the Rabbi, 'and blessed be his holy name for ever.'"

We should esteem it a mark of honor and peculiar regard, if the king should choose one of our children to be taken into his family, and trained for the throne. There are thousands of little children besides ours, whom God might have taken, if he had been pleased; but he loved ours so much, and loved us so much, that he came into our humble household, and gently bore away from our arms our infant child, and took him into his own family, and placed him among the brightest and best, and made him a king. There is love in that—precious love—a Father's love.

There is love in thus chastising us when we wander, and He would draw us back. I have seen a shepherd striving to drive his flock into the fold, while they would refuse to enter, and prefer to run off into the highways, where they were in danger of being torn and lost. At length, when wearied with efforts to urge them in, he takes a lamb into his arms, and folds it gently in his bosom, and walks into the inclosure, while the mother follows, and the whole flock come on, and are soon folded in the place of safety and peace. So have I seen a family whom God would win to his house and home in heaven; but they became worldly-minded, and wandered away among the dangerous paths of a deceitful, unsatisfying earth; and when his calls and commands had been lost upon them, he has taken their lamb, their pet lamb, their youngest child, and laid it in his own bosom; and then, O then, how readily the mother and all the little flock have followed him to the gate of the celestial city, into which he has entered with their darling in his arms!

It was love, infinite love, that ordered such a plan; and it will be felt the more, the more the heart is softened, and the eyes are opened to behold the hand that does it.

"Before I was afflicted, I went astray." "It is good for me that I have been afflicted." So David was able to say while yet in the house of his pilgrimage; and so shall we say, if not now, when we come to sit down by the river of the water of life, our children with us, broken households reunited, and talk over the trials of the way by which we have been led, and admire and adore the grace that directed the blow that laid our early hopes in ruins, blasted our fond domestic joys, buried our babes, and broke our hearts.

CHAPTER VI.

𝔗𝔥𝔢 𝔆𝔥𝔦𝔩𝔡 𝔦𝔰 𝔥𝔞𝔭𝔭𝔦𝔢𝔯 𝔫𝔬𝔴.

WE desire our children's happiness; we pray and labor for it; we are willing to make great sacrifices of our comfort to secure it for them. In sickness, we forget our own health and lives for the sake of theirs. We watch them, and toil for them, and would die for them. We more than die for them sometimes.

And if we grieve when their happiness calls them from us, our grief is selfish; it is for ourselves, and not for them, we mourn. But we should not mourn, if we knew what he has gained whom we have lost. Instantly on being released from the body, the spirit of the infant returns to God who gave it. Endowed with capacities that, if permitted to expand and improve on earth, would in fifty years, perhaps, have made him wiser than Newton, or Plato, or Solomon, it rushes into the mysteries of the divine Mind, and, on wings of thought such as angels use in rising into the regions of knowledge that pass all understanding, he begins his flight, and stretches onward and right onward for ever. He never tires. No weakness, no sickness, no pain, to make him pause or falter in his upward way. He bears himself into the presence of the Omniscient, becomes a disciple in the school of Christ, flies on with Moses, and David, and John, and learns from them the wonderful things of heaven, the mysteries of the kingdom; and thus, ever advancing, he rises nearer and still nearer to the comprehension of Him who is still infinitely above and beyond his last and loftiest reach. And what a change is this! Yesterday, an infant in his mother's arms, or a child amused with a rattle or a straw; to-day, a seraph in the midst of seraphim, burning with excessive glory in the presence of God.

Happiness is the fruit of holiness. Washed in the blood of the everlasting covenant, and sanctified by the Holy Ghost, he is now among the holy, as happy as any who are there. Those faculties of mind, expanded in the atmosphere of heaven, are employed in the praise of that grace that called him so soon from Nature's darkness into the glorious light of *eternity;* the gloom of sin scarce shading the brightness of his rising sun, before the

noon of heaven burst upon him. As if an
angel had lost his way, and for a few days had
wandered among the sons of men, till his
companions suddenly discovered him in this
wilderness, and caught him, and bore him off
to his native residence among the blessed; so
the child is taken kindly in the morning of
its wanderings, and gathered among the holy,
and brought home to his Father's house. How
pure his spirit now; how happy he is now!

> "Apostles, martyrs, prophets, there
> Around my Saviour stand;"

and among them I behold the infant forms
of those whose little graves were wet with the
tears of parental love. I hear their infant
voices in the song. Do you see in the midst
of that bright and blessed throng the child
you mourn? I ask not now if you would
call him back again. I fear you would!
But I ask you, "*What would tempt him back
again?*" Bring out the playthings that he
loved on earth, the toys that filled his childish
heart with gladness, and pleased him on the
nursery floor, the paradise that was ever
bright when he smiled within it; hold them
up, and ask him to throw away his harp, and
leave the side of his new-found friends, and

the bosom of his Saviour; and would he come, to be a boy again, to live and laugh and love again, to sicken, suffer, die, and *perhaps* be lost! I think he would stay. I think I would shut the door if I saw him coming.

A father, who had buried the youngest of three boys, exclaims, in words familiar:

"I cannot tell what form is his,
  What look he weareth now,
Nor guess how bright a glory crowns
  His shining seraph-brow.

"The thoughts that fill his sinless soul,
  The bliss that he doth feel,
Are numbered with the secret things
  Which God doth not reveal.

"But I know—for God hath told me this—
  That now he is at rest,
Where other blessed infants are,
  On their loving Saviour's breast.

"Whate'er befalls his brethren twain,
  His bliss can never cease;
Their lot may here be grief and pain,
  But his is perfect peace.

"It may be that the tempter's wiles
  Their souls from bliss can sever;
But if our own poor faith fail not,
  He must be ours for ever.

"When we think of what our darling is,
   And what he still must be;
When we think on that world's perfect bliss,
   And this world's misery;

"When we groan beneath this load of sin,
   And feel this grief and pain;
Oh! we'd rather lose our other two,
   Than have him here again."

CHAPTER VII.

𝔚e shall see him again.

"I SHALL go to him, but he shall not return to me."

"Shall we know our friends in heaven?" is a question that I will not here discuss. It is to my mind obvious that the personality of each of us is to be preserved distinctly in the world to come; and whether the ties that are formed on earth are to be reunited and perpetuated there, or not, we shall undoubtedly recognize the spirit allied to our own, and that once breathed the same vital air with us. Those who have died in Christ, the Saviour will bring with him; and those who wait his appearance shall meet those they loved, when they come in the air with their glorified Lord.

Very true it is, that the Lamb in the midst of the throne is the chief attraction of heaven, and that all eyes and all hearts will turn toward him with infinite longings that are never satisfied.

A pious young man, of ardent filial affection, buried his beloved mother, and afterwards was frequently heard to say, that one of the chief pleasures he anticipated in the prospect of heaven was meeting again his sainted mother. But that young man, on his death-bed, was heard to say, "It seems to me, if I am so happy as to enter heaven, that I shall wish to spend a thousand years, before I think of any thing else, in looking upon my Saviour."

Yes, blessed Saviour; and in thy bosom nestles the lamb from our fold. We cannot look at thee, without beholding him. We cannot think of him, without remembering thy sweet words, "Suffer the little children to come unto me."

It is not, then, the illusion of fancy, it is the dictate of Christian faith, to look toward the holy city, and within its gates of pearl to see the little one that has been taken from us, now a pure beatified spirit, robed in celestial beauty, with a crown on his head, and a harp in his hand, beckoning us to come up thither.

Oh! it was sweet to hear his voice in the glee of infancy; to feel his lips as they pressed the fount of life, or met our own in the kiss

of parental love ; to listen to his infant prayer,
or his gentle murmur, when we hummed the
evening lullaby.

> "His presence was like sunshine,
> Sent down to gladden earth ;
> To comfort us in all our griefs,
> And sweeten all our mirth."

But he is brighter, fairer, happier there ;
and we shall soon rejoin him in our Father's
house, a reunited family, all the more blessed
because we have been for a little while sepa-
rated, and then we shall part no more for ever.
This is the comfort of faith, the assurance of
hope ; and when we come to sit down in the
mansions on high, with our children around
us, those children over whose early graves we
wept in bitterness, we shall be amazed to
think how short has been the separation, and
how blessed the love that ordered the parting, and permitted the meeting, in the presence of God.

> "Oh! when a mother meets on high
> The babe she lost in infancy,
> Hath she not then, for pains and fears,
> The day of wo, the watchful night,
> For all her sorrows, all her tears,
> An over-payment of delight?"

CHAPTER VIII.

Letter from a Friend.

" MY DEAR FRIEND :—I have just heard of your bereavement, and hasten to offer you my Christian sympathies. I know, indeed, that no creature can give you effectual comfort, nor do I propose to do for you any office which might not be performed by the humblest servant of Christ. The sooner you look away from earth, and set your hope in God, the better for you. He is our buckler, and shield, and salvation. He is a very present help in time of trouble. Compared with our necessities, or with God, all earthly friends and resources are poor things. " Cease from man, whose breath is in his nostrils." Sometimes the very tears of our friends, by showing us how vain is human aid, deepen our sorrows.

"Our heavenly Father is full of kindness, mercy, and grace. He does not afflict willingly. He is a sun and shield ; he will give grace and glory ; and no good thing will he withhold from them that walk uprightly.

'There is more comfort in one drop that distils from God, than from ten thousand rivers that flow from creature delights.' Are you an heir of God, and a joint-heir with Christ? then 'Behold what manner of love the Father hath bestowed upon us, that we should be called the sons of God!' Have you not a good Father?

"And is not Jesus the very friend you need? To all his people he is of old a Redeemer and Saviour. 'In all their affliction he was afflicted, and the angel of his presence saved them.' He says, 'Let not your heart be troubled, neither let it be afraid; ye believe in God, believe also in me.' He well knows what sorrow means. He has felt the keenest pangs. He never breaks the bruised reed. He was sent to bind up the broken-hearted, and to comfort all that mourn. If we suffer with him, we shall also reign with him. Blessed Saviour! thou hast said, 'Because I live, ye shall live also.' At thy bidding I would bear all things. I had rather be with thee in a dungeon, than with thy foes in a palace. Let me, in my measure, fill up that which is behind of thy sufferings. In due time thou wilt make all things plain. Let me but at last be with thee, and I will rejoice in tribulation. Let my sins be surely pardoned through thy blood, and I will yield to no fear; and then

'The glory of my glory still shall be,
To give all glory and myself to Thee.'

"He will not leave you comfortless. It is the very office of his Spirit to cheer and encourage our hearts. How marvellously can this Spirit of love and of holiness chase away our darkness! He giveth songs in the night. He is the oil of gladness. His grace, and pity, and love are infinite, eternal, and unchangeable. Get the help of the Spirit, and nothing can undo you.

"This is the very time for you to plead and rest upon the provisions of that covenant which is ordered in all things and sure, which is both new and everlasting, which is sealed with blood, confirmed with an oath, established upon the best of promises, and ordained in the hands of a Mediator who cannot fail nor be discouraged. In this covenant is no flaw. Under it there can be no failure. Rest in it, yea, glory in it, and remember all it promises and secures.

"But still you weep for your little one. Blessed be God, it is no sin to weep. Jesus wept. Yet, while nature pours out her tears, let grace triumph. I have long thought that the grief of God's children for the death of their infant offspring should be very moderate. The view taken of the state of such by the best Reformed Churches, has always been cheering. Hear the Synod of Dort: 'Seeing that we are to judge of the will of God by his Word, which testifies that the children of believers are holy, not indeed by nature, but by the benefit of the gracious covenant, in which they are comprehended along with their parents, pious parents ought not to doubt of the election and salvation of their children whom God hath called in infancy out of this life.' And our own Confession very clearly and delightfully states *how* they are saved: 'Elect infants, dying in infancy, are regenerated and saved by Christ, through the Spirit, who worketh when, and where, and how he pleaseth.' If, therefore, you still weep, weep as one full of hope, and peace, and comfort.

"Your present trial will furnish you with many an occasion of showing your readiness to perform two duties united by the Psalmist: '*Trust in the Lord,* and *do good.*' It can hardly be doubted that, great as your affliction is, you can easily find others who need your sympathy and aid.' Visit them; write to them; speak comfortably to them; weep with them; if they need it, give them alms; in short, be as useful as you can. In watering others, you shall be watered. Beware of moping over your trials.

"It is a painful but universal conviction among Christians, that they need correction. Their tempers, their tongues, their lives, their inconstancy, all show that fewer chastisements would leave them in a sad state. I know not what the Lord would accomplish in you by this heavy stroke; but sure I am that he would cause all things to work together for good to them that love him. You have found former trials good. This, too, shall yield the peaceable fruit of righteousness.

"And as to your loved one, has not God already done for it more than you and all the world could have done in a thousand years? He has made it a king and a priest unto God, to serve him day and night in heaven. If Hannah was willing to give up Samuel to serve in the earthly tabernacle, surely you should be willing to resign your darling to serve in the temple not made with hands, especially as you hope so soon to follow him, and be for ever with him.

"At most, will not all this darkness soon be gone? 'Weeping may endure for a night, but joy cometh in the morning.' 'It is but a little while, and he that shall come will come, and will not tarry.' 'The time is short.' Let us wait patiently for him. His deliverances are as seasonable as they are effectual. When you reach the blessed home above, you will be the first to say that God hath done all things well.

"And now, if the tempter should annoy and insult you, saying God has forsaken you, believe him not, but say, 'Rejoice not against me, O mine enemy; when I fall, I shall arise; when I sit in darkness, the Lord shall be a light unto me. I will bear the indignation of the Lord, because I have sinned against him, until he plead my cause, and execute judgment for me. He will bring me forth to the light, and I shall behold his righteousness.'

"Very truly yours,

"W. S. P."

CHAPTER IX.

Two Years in Heaven.

Two years ago to-day he went to heaven.

With us they have been long, long years, since we heard the sound of his sweet voice, and the merry laugh that burst from his glad heart.

He was the youngest of our flock. Three summers he had been with us, and oh! he was brighter and sunnier than any summer day of them all. But he died as the third year of his life was closing. The others were older than he; and all we had of childhood's glee and gladness was buried when we laid him in the grave. Since then our hearth has been desolate, and our hearts have been yearning for the boy who is gone. *"Gone, but not lost,"* we have said a thousand times; and we think of him ever as living and blessed in another place not far from us.

Two years in heaven! They do not measure *time* in that world; there are no weeks, or months, or years; but all the time we have been mourning his absence here, he has been happy there. And when we think of what he has been enjoying, and the rapid progress he has been making, we feel that it is well for him that he has been taken away.

Two years with angels! They have been his constant companions, his teachers too; and from them he has drawn lessons of knowledge and of love. The cherubim are said to excel in knowledge; while love glows more ardently in the breasts of seraphim. He has been two years in the company of both, and must have become very like them.

Two years with the redeemed! They have told him of the Saviour, in whose blood they washed their robes, and whose righteousness is their salvation. The child, while with us, knew little of Jesus and his dying love; but he has heard of him now, and has learned to love him who said, "Suffer little children to come unto me." There are some among those redeemed, who would have loved him here, had they been living with us; but they went to glory before him, and have welcomed him now to their company. I am not sure that they know him as our child; and yet do we love to think that he is in the arms of those who have gone from our arms, and that thus broken families are reunited around the throne of God and the Lamb.

Two years with Christ! It is joy to know that our child has been two years with the Saviour, in his immediate presence; learning of him, and making heaven vocal with songs of rapture and love. The blessed Saviour took little children in his arms when he was here on earth, and he takes them in his bosom there. Blessed Jesus! blessed children! blessed child!

He often wept when he was with us; he suffered much before he died: seven days and nights he was torn with fierce convulsions ere his soul yielded and fled to heaven. But now for two years he has not wept. He has known no pain for two years. That little child, who was pleased with a rattle, now meets with angels and feels himself at home. He walks among the tallest spirits that bend in the presence of the Infinite, and is as free and happy as any who are there. And when we think of joys that are his, we are more than willing that he should stay where he now dwells, though our house is darkened by the shadow of his grave, and our hearts are aching all the time for his return. Long and weary have been the years without him; but they have been blessed years to him in heaven. "Even so, Father." "Not our will, but thine be done."

CHAPTER X.

After Years.

TWELVE years and more have passed since the preceding pages were first published. They have been abroad in the world on a mission of consolation, and oh! how many hearts have been soothed in sorrow, and comforted by the ministry of these words!

Again they are to go on their errand of mercy. The heart from which they first went out has found that the words of Jesus are indeed true, "Blessed are they that mourn, for they shall be comforted." The Saviour is the great healer, and he takes time to work his sovereign cures. He leads his followers in paths they know not, and purifies them for himself by trials such as they would not choose. He prayed for himself, that if it were possible the cup might pass from him, but it pleased his Father that he should drink it to the dregs. And if he could not be spared, should his children murmur when they are called to taste the bitter waters of affliction? In time, and if not in time, certainly in eternity, they will see that it is more than good to be afflicted, and the best of all the means employed for their sanctification were the sorrows through which they were called to pass.

And as these twelve years and more have been wearing away, the sorrow that gave birth to these pages has become a more hallowed, chastened, and gentle emotion. The child of our affections is advancing in the beauty and blessedness and glory of the heavenly state, and daily becomes more at home among the angels and saints. Others whom we love have gone there and joined the company of the redeemed, and we think of our child, a child indeed, but a companion of our departed and now glorified friends. More and more willing are we that he should stay where he is. More and more do we long to be absent from the body and present with the Lord.

An unknown friend, in the midst of deep personal affliction, heard the following sentences fall from the lips of Rev. Dr. P. D. Gurley, in his pulpit in Washington City, and when I learned how full of consolation and truth they were, I asked the privilege of repeating them here.

———

It is God who has taken your loved one away. It was not an enemy that did it, but a friend; not an erring mortal, but He who sees the end from the beginning, and doeth all things well. Bow at his feet, and say with him who lost his possessions, his servants, and ALL his CHILDREN in a single day, "The Lord gave and the Lord hath taken away." Acknowledge, with unreserved submission, that he has taken but what he gave; that he has only asserted his right as a sovereign, and done what he would with his own. Nay more, confide in his wisdom, confide in his faithfulness, confide in his love. The hour of sorrow is the time for faith to take her boldest flight and achieve her brightest victory. Let her soar above the clouds to the eternal sunshine beyond, the sunshine of a Father's mercy. Perhaps I should rather say, Let her fix her eye upon the bright bow of promise that spans the clouds, and hear the voice that comes down through the darkness and says in words of parental counsel and tenderness: "My son, despise not thou the chastening of the Lord, nor faint when thou art rebuked of him; for whom the Lord loveth, he chasteneth." It is the voice of your heavenly Father, nay more, of your Redeemer and your God. Let it hush every murmuring thought, quiet every rebellious feeling, and call out from your very souls that submissive and memorable utterance of the Saviour: "Even so, Father, for so it seems good in thy sight." "He maketh sore and bindeth up; he woundeth, and his hands make whole." He has smitten, not to repel you, but to draw you nearer to himself. And how must you approach him? Not merely to acknowledge his hand, his sovereignty, his wisdom, and his faithfulness; not merely to supplicate his assistance and his mercy; but to worship and to bless him. Oh! this is the highest triumph of faith and piety—to look up from the depths of affliction, and say not merely, "The Lord gave and the Lord hath taken away"—that *may* be but a cold and heartless acknowledgment— but "Blessed be the name of the Lord;" let him be praised for this very dealing. I needed it, and he, in his loving kindness, has ordered it for my good. Here is the point to which your redeeming God would bring you. Have you reached it yet? If not, then pray,

and pray very earnestly, that you may not
fail to reach it; for that is the point where
trial accomplishes its perfect work, and secures for those who are exercised thereby
"a far more exceeding and eternal weight of
glory."

CHAPTER XI.

A German Mother.

A SMITTEN household in Germany is brought to our sight in this letter from the husband and father. It is highly wrought, but the mother, crushed under the sudden and great sorrow, sees the Saviour and finds peace in leaving her child in his bosom. Blessed trust!

"My wife trembled all over, and sat down with the child in her arms. O God! that can not be true. He will not punish us so cruelly; oh! pray, do pray that he will spare us the child. I took our Prayer-Book and sat down beside the dull lamp. I began, half weeping, to read a prayer for the sick, and read devotionally. 'Ah! not so, Peter, not so,' she said, 'that is of no use, there is nothing about our child in it; pray to him to spare her.' I turned to another prayer and read yet more devotionally. 'Ah! that is no good; pray out of yourself whatever comes into your head, only about the child!' I rose up from the lamp, my heart full of anguish, anguish about the child, anguish that I could not pray. I never had prayed out of my own heart. Then, in her agony, my wife fell upon her knees, and called upon God. O Father! leave us the child, do not take it back again; it shall be thine, shall be our angel and thine, shall be the Saviour's own through all eternity. We will carry it in our hands as thy precious gift; will trouble no more, but will bear all humbly and patiently that thou dost send us; will look for only good from thee. But the child, the child! do not take it; leave it for thy Son's sake.' Fervently she looked upward, the tears streaming over her face, the child in her arms pressed close to her heart. It moved, and as Madeli looked down, it stretched its little limbs once more, opened its eyes full upon its mother, a smile passed over its little face, and then the eyes slowly closed. The smile seemed to wing its way like a little angel from the face, and with it the spirit of the child had departed too! Its body moved no more; its eyes were shut for ever! The mother looked up full of reproach to heaven; the convulsion that had left the heart of the child seemed now to have fastened upon hers. Sobbing violently, she bent over the corpse, seeking for life. When she found no sign, she tottered to the bed, laid the body upon it, and throwing herself over it, was so overcome with anguish that the bed shook under her. Grief seized me, too, as with an iron clutch; but the state of my wife roused me from my stupor. I tried to speak with her, but the convulsion would allow no answer, and I feared each minute that she must be suffocated. At last I succeeded in laying her on the bed, and calming her with water. She would not have the little body moved from her arms, but lay back, silently motioning me to be still, and not torment her with speaking.

"The first beams of the morning found me faint and half-asleep upon a chair; a calm, earnest gaze welcomed them from the bed, as they fell upon Madeli's folded hands and upon the golden curls of our living child. I awoke from my sad dreams, and went out into the kitchen to prepare something warm for us after the night of weeping. But Madeli held me fast, begging me not to go, she had something to say to me. She could not describe to me what she had felt when she first knew the child to be dying in her arms. For the first time in her life the fountain of prayer seemed to be opened within her, and she poured out her soul to the Father in heaven. She felt a strength in her heart as though, if she had asked for a kingdom, that Father must give it her! And when she had finished, the child was dead.

"Then she felt as though a burning hand tore her heart from her body, as though a thousand mountains were hurled down upon her breast, as though an unfathomable abyss opened to swallow her in infinite darkness. Her faith was gone. 'There is no God,' a voice thundered in her heart. An eternal nothingness stared her in the face with nnutterable horror. She clung to the little body that she, too, might become a corpse, and lose consciousness, since man was nothing but a growing corpse, with no God, no living eternity, only an everlasting grave. No one can picture to themselves that terrible sensation, when one thinks one has clung firmly, lovingly to heaven, and is seized, as though by a sudden madness, that there is no God, and every pulse echoes to us the cry: 'There is no God; your faith is vain!' 'For a long time,' said Madeli, 'I did not know if I was alive or dead. I thought nothing: I could only suffer. Gradually consciousness seemed to

return, but for very long I could not find
God.'

"At length it seemed to her as though a
little spark arose, glimmering faintly, giving
out very little light; and in the gleam of this
light she saw again that smile of her child
which had hovered over its face before it left
us. Again the child seemed to live, and to
smile at some one with tenderness and trust.
Up out of the darkness came a form lovely
and tender to look upon, to whom the child
held out its arms. The figure took the child
on its arm, putting its hand on its head. The
child's face seemed to become glorified: it
was as though wings waved from its shoul-
ders, and its eyes turned to the mother, joy-
ful and sparkling like carbuncles! Instantly
Madeli saw that it was the Saviour who held
and blest her child, and as she thought it, he
raised his finger, as though to say, 'Woman,
if thou hadst had faith!' and in that hand
she saw the marks of the nails, and thought
how he, too, had known great sorrow, and
had prayed, 'Father, if it be possible, let this
cup pass from me, yet not my will but thine
be done;' and the cup of sorrow did not pass
from him: he drank it to the last drop, and
he rose again the third day, as a sign that

there is a Father in heaven who can hear and
bless obedience. And as she thought that,
the light grew larger, and glowed like the sun,
and the two forms became more heavenly,
and looked at her with increasing tenderness.
It was as though whole beams of love pene-
trated her heart, and in a splendor which her
eyes could not bear, the Saviour and the
child both vanished away.

"By degrees she became convinced that the
death of the child was not a punishment, but
a voice from God. And as God had so highly honored her as to call her through a little
angel, she would remain consecrated to him;
and she thought she should be able. Thus
was my wife made holy through the child,
who became to her an angel, and who
stretched out to her its little hand across the
threshold which separates the earthly heart
from God; but the angel drew with angelic
power, and the mother passed the threshold
and walked with God; that is, she purified
herself to a holy temple, and fulfilled every
duty in his name, and loved all in his love,
and judged no one herself, but gave them
over to the judgment of Him who says, 'I
will repay.'"

Hymns and Poems.

I SEE that "one is not" in your household, and that you have learned what that Scripture meaneth, "*and so death came by sin.*" Death is a stern teacher, but I trust that you have found new and precious experiences in this new road which you have been called to travel. Count it no strange thing, for this is the King's highway, over which all the ransomed pass. There is not a house where there has not been one dead; and if your house be desolate, let your heart be full of glad thanksgivings that it is "*the Lord who gave, and the Lord who has taken away.*" You have now new attractions in the eternal world to draw your hearts thither. Every thing is moving on to higher conditions, and your own hearts should be constantly going upwards. May God give you grace, and fill you with his peace!

ERRATA.

The additions to this volume consist of about ten new pages of prose matter, and fifteen of poetry : the printer, however, neglected to repage the volume beyond the first 70 pages, and pages 61 to 70 are repeated at the beginning of the poetical selections.

Hymns and Poems.

The Dying Child.

INSCRIBED TO MR. AND MRS. S. I. PRIME, ON THE
DEATH OF THEIR YOUNGEST SON.

How calm, how beautiful he lies!
'Neath drooping fringes shine his eyes,
    Like stars in half eclipse;
As sunlight falls his wavy hair
Across that noble brow, so fair,
That the blue veins seem penciled there,
    And curved by Art those lips.

No quivering of the lid or chin
Betrays the final strife within;
    So noiseless sinks his breath,
That if those cheeks did not disclose
Life's current in the tint of rose
That, like a bright thought, comes and goes,
    This would seem beauteous death.

Already is the stain of earth—
The stamp of his terrestrial birth—
     Changing for heaven's pure seal:
The angel's beauty now I see
Pledged in that sweet serenity;
And that unearthly smile to me
     God's signet doth reveal.

But even here his guileless life—
His path with only flowerets rife—
     Almost a cherub's seemed:
He knew no change from light to shade,
His soul its own glad sunshine made;
Where'er he paused, where'er he strayed,
     Light all around him beamed.

If such hath been his life's first dawn,
Oh, what will be the glorious morn
     Just opening on his soul!
Favored of Heaven! to wear the crown,
Life's weary race to thee unknown,
And sit with laureled conquerors down,
     Who toiled to reach the goal.

But fading is that roseate hue;
And now cold pearly drops bedew
     That brow of heavenly mould;
Fainter and fainter grows his breath:
Ah, now 'tis gone!   Can this be death?
Oh, what so fair the heavens beneath,
     So lovely to behold!

Newark, October 29, 1849.   E. C. K.

Suspiria.

TAKE them, O Death! and bear away
 Whatever thou canst call thine own!
Thine image, stamped upon this clay,
 Doth give thee that, but that alone!

Take them, O Grave! and let them lie
 Folded upon thy narrow shelves,
As garments by the soul laid by,
 And precious only to ourselves!

Take them, O great Eternity!
 Our little life is but a gust,
That bends the branches of thy tree,
 And trails its blossoms in the dust!

LONGFELLOW.

Bereabement.

NAY, weep not, dearest, though the child be dead ;
　He lives again in heaven's unclouded life,
With other angels that have early fled
　From the dark scenes of sorrow, sin, and strife ;
Nay, weep not, dearest, though thy yearning love
　Would fondly keep for earth its fairest flowers,
And e'en deny to brighter realms above
　The few that deck this dreary world of ours.
Though much it seems a wonder and a woe
　That one so loved should be so early lost,
And hallowed tears may unforbidden flow
　To mourn the blossom that we cherished most—
Yet all is well : GOD's good design I see,
That where our treasure is, our hearts may be !

JOHN G. SAXE.

On Seeing a Deceased Infant.

AND this is death! How cold and still,
  And yet how lovely it appears!
Too cold to let the gazer smile,
  And yet too beautiful for tears.
The sparkling eye no more is bright,
  The cheek has lost its rose-like red;
And yet it is with strange delight
  I stand and gaze upon the dead.

But when I see the fair, wide brow,
  Half shaded by the silken hair,
That never looked so fair as now
  When life and health were laughing there,
I wonder not that grief should swell
  So wildly upward in the breast,
And that strong passion once rebel
  That need not, cannot be suppressed.

I wonder not that parents' eyes,
  In gazing thus, grow cold and dim;
That burning tears and aching sighs
  Are blended with the funeral hymn:
The spirit hath an earthly part,
  That weeps when earthly pleasure flies;
And Heaven would scorn the frozen heart
  That melts not when the infant dies.

And yet why mourn? That deep repose
  Shall never more be broke by pain;
Those lips no more in sighs unclose,
  Those eyes shall never weep again.
For think not that the blushing flower
  Shall wither in the churchyard sod;
'Twas made to gild an angel's bower
  Within the Paradise of God.

Once more I gaze, and swift and far
  The clouds of death in sorrow fly;
I see thee, like a new-born star,
  Move up thy pathway in the sky:
The star hath rays serene and bright,
  But cold and pale compared with thine;
For thy orb shines with heavenly light,
  With beams unfading and divine.

Then let the burthened heart be free,
  The tears of sorrow all be shed,
And parents calmly bend to see
  The mournful beauty of the dead:
Thrice happy, that their infant bears
  To heaven no darkening stains of sin;
And only breathed life's morning airs,
  Before its noonday storms begin.

Farewell! I shall not soon forget!
  Although thy heart hath ceased to beat,
My memory warmly treasures yet
  Thy features calm and mildly sweet.

But no ; that look is not the last :
  We yet may meet where seraphs dwell,
Where love no more deplores the past,
  Nor breathes that withering word—Farewell.

W. O. B. Peabody.

The Early Lost.

Wʜᴇɴ the soft airs and quickening showers
  Of spring-time make the meadows green,
And clothe the sunny hills with flowers,
  And the cool hollows scooped between,
Ye go, and fondly bending where
  The bloom is brighter than the day,
Ye pluck the loveliest blossom there
  Of all that gem the rich array.
The stem, thus robbed and rudely pressed,
  Stands desolate in the purple even ;
The flower has withered on your breast,
  But given its perfume up to heaven.

When, mid our hopes that waken fears,
  And mid our joys that end in gloom,
The children of our earthly years
  Around us spring, and bud, and bloom,
An angel from the blest above
  Comes down among them at their play,
And takes the one that most we love,
  And bears it silently away :
Bereft, we feel the spirit's strife ;
  But while the inmost soul is riven,
Our dear and beauteous bud of life
  Receives immortal bloom in heaven.

W. D. Gallagher.

The Reaper and the Flowers.

There is a Reaper whose name is Death,
  And with his sickle keen
He reaps the bearded grain at a breath,
  And the flowers that grow between.

" Shall I have naught that is fair ?" saith he,
  " Have naught but the bearded grain ?
Though the breath of these flowers is sweet to me
  I will give them all back again."

He gazed on the flowers with tearful eyes,
  He kissed their drooping leaves :
It was for the Lord of Paradise
  He bound them in his sheaves.

" My Lord hath need of these flowerets gay,"
  The Reaper said, and smiled ;
" Dear tokens of the earth are they,
  Where he was once a child.

" They all shall bloom in fields of light,
  Transplanted by my care ;
And saints upon their garments white
  These sacred flowers wear."

And the mother gave, with tears and pain,
  The flowers she most did love ;
But she knew she should find them all again
  In the fields of light above.

Oh ! not in cruelty, not in wrath
  The Reaper came that day ;
'Twas an angel visited the green earth,
  And took the flowers away.

LONGFELLOW.

The Sculptured Children on Chantrey's Monument at Litchfield.

FAIR images of sleep!
Hallowed, and soft, and deep;
On whose calm lids the dreamy quiet lies,
Like moonlight on shut bells
Of flowers in mossy dells,
Filled with the hush of night and summer skies.

How many hearts have felt
Your silent beauty melt
Their strength to gushing tenderness away!
How many sudden tears,
From depths of buried years,
All freshly bursting, have confessed your sway!

How many eyes will shed
Still, o'er your marble bed,
Such drops, from Memory's troubled fountain
    wrung!
While Hope hath blights to bear,
While Love breathes mortal air,
While roses perish ere to glory sprung.

Yet, from a voiceless home,
If some sad mother come
To bend and linger o'er your lonely rest,

As o'er the cheek's warm glow,
And the soft breathing low
Of babes, that grew and faded on her breast;

If then the dove-like tone
Of those faint murmurs gone,
O'er her sick sense too piercing to return;
If for the soft bright hair,
And brow and bosom fair,
And life, now dust, her soul too deeply yearn;

O gentle forms, entwined
Like tendrils, which the wind
May wave, so clasped, but never can unlink,
Send from your calm profound
A still, small voice, a sound
Of hope, forbidding that lone heart to sink.

By all the pure, meek mind
Of your pale beauty shrined,
By childhood's love—too bright a bloom to die—
O'er her worn spirit shed,
O fairest, holiest dead!
The Faith, Trust, Light o' Immortality!

MRS. HEMANS.

On the Death of a Child.

As the sweet flower that scents the morn,
 But withers in the rising day,
Thus lovely seemed the infant's dawn,
 Thus swiftly fled his life away.

Ere sin could blight or sorrow fade,
 Death timely came with friendly care,
The opening bud to heaven conveyed,
 And bade it bloom for ever there.

Yet the sad hour that took the boy
 Perhaps has spared a heavier doom,
Snatched him from scenes of guilty joy,
 Or from the pangs of ills to come.

He died before his infant soul
 Had ever burned with wrong desire,
Had ever spurned at Heaven's control,
 Or madly quenched its sacred fire.

He died to sin, he died to care,
 But for a moment felt the rod;
Then, springing on the noiseless air,
 Spread his light wings, and soared to God.

    Belfast Selection of Hymns.

On the Death of an Infant.

Why dost thou weep?   Say, can it be
Because, for ever blest, and free
From sin, from sorrow, and from pain,
Thy babe shall never weep again;
Shall never feel, shall never know
Even half thy little load of wo?

What was thy prayer, when his first smile
Did thy young mother-heart beguile;
When his first cry was in thine ear,
And on thy cheek his first warm tear,
And to thy heart at first were pressed
The throbbings of his little breast?

What was thy prayer?   Canst thou not now
See in his bright cherubic brow,
Hear in his soft seraphic strain,
So full of joy, so free from pain,
An answer, (as if God did speak,)
To all thy love had dared to seek?

Why, wherefore weep, when all the cares,
The doubts, the troubles, and the snares,
The threatening clouds, the falling tears,
Childhood's wild hopes, and manhood's fears,
That might have been for him, for thee,
Have passed away, and ne'er shall be?

He scarcely suffered, then was crowned ;
Was scarcely lost till he was found ;
And scarcely heaved one mortal sigh,
Then entered immortality :
A child of thine, a child of bliss !
Why, wherefore weep for joy like this ?

Nay, rather strive to praise the love
That could so tenderly reprove ;
That, when it wounded, left no sting
Of self-consuming suffering ;
But with thy profit linked the joy
Of thy beloved and sainted boy.

J. S. MONSELL.

Mine Earthly Children Round Me Bloom.

MINE earthly children round me bloom,
　　Lovely alike in smiles and tears;
My fairest sleeps within the tomb,　　.
　　Through long and silent years.

And earthly ties are round me wound,
　　And earthly feelings fondly nursed;
And yet the spell is not unbound
　　That linked me to my first—my first!

A fairy thing with flaxen hair,
　　And eyes of blue, and downy cheek,
And frolic limbs, and lips that were
　　Striving for evermore to speak;

A thing as lovely as the day;
　　Fair as the shapes that span the beams;
As innocent as flowers of May;
　　As frail, as fading as our dreams.

I see the seals of childhood fade
　　Slowly from each young living brow;
Yet still, in sunshine and in shade,
　　That infant is an infant now.

Seasons may roll, and manhood's pride
　　Each youthful breast with care may fill;

And one by one they'll leave my side,
   But she will be my baby still.

And every where, by thee unseen,
   That vision followeth every where :
When three are gathered on the green,
   I always see another there.

When three around the board are set,
   And call on father and on mother,
To mortal eyes but three are met ;
   But I—but I can see another.

A cherub child, with angel wings,
   Is floating o'er me fond and free ;
And still that gladsome infant sings,
   "Grieve not, dear mother, not for me."

ELEANOR LEE.

The Child and Death.

"DEAR mother," said a little child,
  "I should not like to die,
And lie within the grave, nor see
  The sun shine in the sky.

"Oh ! is it not a dreadful thought,
  When all the earth is bright,
To know that we must go to sleep,
  And never see the light ?"

"It would be so," the mother said,
  "Were not God's promise given,
That from the dreamless sleep of death
  We shall awake in heaven,

"Where shines a brighter sun than this,
  Our opening eyes to bless,
That never sets, nor veils His face,
  The Sun of Righteousness."

"But does it not seem very sad
  To leave the glad young flowers,
That we have loved to look upon
  Through all the summer hours ?

"When winter comes with threatening clouds,
  They droop their heads and die :
Dear mother, do they live again,
  And blossom in the sky ?"

" Not so, my child.   Like us, the flowers
　　Of earthly dust are made ;
But heaven has skies without a cloud,
　　And flowers that never fade.

"And happy spirits wander there
　　Through long, unnumbered days,
And join the angels round the throne
　　In songs of endless praise."

" Dear mother," said the little child,
　　With earnest, thoughtful eye,
And drawing closer to her side,
　　" How I should *like to die !*"

SUSAN PINDAR.

The Dying Child.

"Mother, I'm tired, and I would fain be sleeping;
  Let me repose upon thy bosom seek;
But promise me that thou wilt leave off weeping,
  Because thy tears fall hot upon my cheek.
Here it is cold; the tempest raveth madly:
  But in my dreams all is so wondrous bright;
I see the angel children smiling gladly,
  When from my weary eyes I shut the light.

"Mother, one steals beside me now! And listen:
  Dost thou not hear the music's sweet accord?
See how his white wings beautifully glisten!
  Surely those wings were given him by our Lord!
Green, gold, and red are floating all around me;
  They are the flowers the angel scattereth:
Shall I have also wings whilst life has bound me?
  Or, mother, are they given alone in death?

"Why dost thou clasp me as if I were going?
  Why dost thou press thy cheek thus unto mine?
Thy cheek is hot, and still thy tears are flowing:
  I will, dear mother, will be always thine!
Do not sigh thus; it marreth my reposing;
  And if thou weep, then I must weep with thee.
Oh, I am tired; my weary eyes are closing:
  Look, mother, look! the angel kisseth me!"

FROM THE DANISH OF ANDERSON.

Willy.

Quiet slumberer!   No gleam
Of fretful fancy, thought, or dream,
Passes over Death's calm stream
    To thee, Willy.

Though our tears are flowing free,
Though we sorrow sore for thee,
Thou art happier than we
    In heaven, Willy.

Stricken from this weary life
Ere the world began its strife,
Or its toils and cares were rife
    With thee, Willy;

Time has brought no bitter thing,
Death no terror and no sting;
Angel bands are hovering
    O'er thee, Willy.

FROM " CAPRICES."

Resigning.

"Poor heart! what bitter words we speak
When God speaks of resigning!"

CHILDREN, that lay their pretty garlands by
Most lingeringly, yet with a patient will;
Sailors, that, when the o'erladen ship lies still,
Cast out her precious freight with veiléd eye,
Riches for life exchanging solemnly,
Lest they should never reach the wished-for shore:
Thus we, O Infinite! stand thee before,
And lay down at Thy feet, without one sigh,
Each after each, our lovely things and rare,
Our close heart-jewels and our garlands fair.
Perhaps Thou knewest that the flowers would die,
And the long-voyaged hoards be found all dust;
So take them while unchanged. To Thee we trust
For incorruptible treasure—Thou art just.

A Sunbeam and a Shadow.

I.

I HEAR a shout of merriment,
  A laughing boy I see;
Two little feet the carpet press,
  And bring the child to me.

Two little arms are round my neck,
  Two feet upon my knee:
How fall the kisses on my cheek;
  How sweet they are to me!

II.

That merry shout no more I hear,
  No laughing child I see;
No little arms are round my neck,
  Nor feet upon my knee!

No kisses drop upon my cheek;
  Those lips are sealed to me.
Dear Lord, how could I give him up
  To any but to Thee!

The Dying Boy.

It must be sweet in childhood to give back
The spirit to its Maker, ere the heart
Has grown familiar with the paths of sin,
And sown—to garner up its bitter fruits!
I knew a boy, whose infant feet had trod
Upon the blossoms of some seven springs;
And when the eighth came round, and called him
  out
To revel in its light, he turned away,
And sought his chamber, to lie down and die.
'Twas night: he summoned his accustomed friends,
And on this wise bestowed his last bequest:

  Mother, I'm dying now!
There's a deep suffocation in my breast,
As if some heavy hand my bosom pressed;
  And on my brow

  I feel the cold sweat stand;
My lips grow dry and tremulous, and my breath
Comes feebly up.   Oh, tell me, is this death?
  Mother, your hand!

  Here! lay it on my wrist,
And place the other thus beneath my head:
And say, sweet mother, say, when I am dead
  Shall I be missed?

Never beside your knee
Shall I kneel down again at night to pray;
Nor with the morning wake, and sing the lay
    You taught to me.

Oh, at the time of prayer,
When you look round and see a vacant seat,
You will not wait then for my coming feet!
    You'll miss me there.

Father, I'm going home,
To the good home you spoke of; that blest land
Where it is one bright summer always, and
    Storms never come.

I must be happy then:
From pain and death you say I shall be free;
That sickness never enters there; and we
    Shall meet again.

Brother, the little spot
I used to call *my* garden, where long hours
We've staid to watch the budding things and flowers,
    Forget it not!

Plant there some box or pine;
Something that lives in winter, and will be
A verdant offering to my memory;
    And call it mine.

Sister, my young rose tree,
That all the spring has been my pleasant care,
Just putting forth its leaves, so green and fair,
    I give to thee.

    And when its roses bloom,
I shall be gone away, my short life done.
But will you not bestow a single one
    Upon my tomb?

    Now, mother, sing the tune
You sung last night; I'm weary, and must sleep.
Who was it called my name? Nay, do nct weep;
    You'll all come soon!

Morning spread o'er the earth her rosy wings,
And that meek sufferer, cold and ivory pale,
Lay on his couch asleep. The gentle air
Came through the open window, freighted with
The savory odors of the early spring:
He breathed it not. The laugh of passers-by
Jarred like a discord in some mournful tune,
But wakened not his slumbers. He was dead!

              J. H. BRIGHT.

Little Bessie:

AND THE WAY IN WHICH SHE FELL ASLEEP.

Hug me closer, closer, mother,
　Put your arms around me tight;
I am cold and tired, mother,
　And I feel so strange to-night!
Something hurts me here, dear mother,
　Like a stone upon my breast;
Oh, I wonder, wonder, mother,
　Why it is I cannot rest!

All the day, while you were working,
　As I lay upon my bed,
I was trying to be patient,
　And to think of what you said;
How the kind and blessed Jesus
　Loves his lambs to watch and keep;
And I wished he'd come and take me
　In his arms, that I might sleep.

Just before the lamp was lighted,
　Just before the children came,
While the room was very quiet,
　I heard some one call my name.
All at once the window opened;
　In a field were lambs and sheep;
Some from out a brook were drinking,
　Some were lying fast asleep.

But I could not see the Saviour,
   Though I strained my eyes to see;
And I wondered, if he saw me,
   Would he speak to such as me.
In a moment I was looking
   On a world so bright and fair,
Which was full of little children,
   And they seemed so happy there!

They were singing, oh, how sweetly!
   Sweeter songs I never heard;
They were singing sweeter, mother,
   Than our little yellow-bird.
And while I my breath was holding,
   One, so bright, upon me smiled;
And I knew it must be Jesus,
   When he said, "Come here, my child.

"Come up here, my little Bessie,
   Come up here and live with me,
Where the children never suffer,
   But are happier than you see!"
Then I thought of all you'd told me
   Of that bright and happy land:
I was going when you called me,
   When you came and kissed my hand.

And at first I felt so sorry
   You had called me: I would go.

Oh, to sleep and never suffer!
　Mother, don't be crying so!
Hug me closer, closer, mother,
　Put your arms around me tight;
Oh, how much I love you, mother,
　But I feel so strange to-night!

And the mother pressed her closer
　To her overburdened breast;
On the heart so near to breaking
　Lay the heart so near its rest.
At the solemn hour of midnight,
　In the darkness calm and deep,
Lying on her mother's bosom,
　Little Bessie fell asleep.　　　　R.

The New-Year's Eve.*

If you're waking, call me early, call me early,
  mother dear,
For I would see the sun rise upon the glad New-
  Year:
It is the last New-Year that I shall ever see,
Then you may lay me low i' the mould, and think
  no more of me.

To-night I saw the sun set; he set and left behind
The good old year, the dear old time, and all my
  peace of mind;
Now the New-Year's coming up, mother, but I shall
  never see
The blossom on the blackthorn, the leaf upon the
  tree.

Last May we made a crown of flowers; we had a
  merry day;
Beneath the hawthorn on the green they made me
  Queen of May;

---

* The second and concluding part of that exquisite
poem of Tennyson's, The May Queen, is here inserted
entire, with the exception of one verse. Although not
referring to the death of a young child, it possesses a tender interest to every bereaved parent.

And we danced about the May-pole, and in the hazel
copse,
Till Charles's Wain* came out above the tall white
chimney-tops.

There's not a flower on all the hills: the frost is on
the pane:
I only wish to live till the snowdrops come again:
I wish the snow would melt, and the sun come out
on high:
I long to see a flower so, before the day I die.

The building rook 'll caw in the windy tall elm tree,
And the tufted plover pipe along the fallow lea,
And the swallow 'll come back again, with summer,
o'er the wave,
But I shall lie alone, mother, within the mouldering
grave!

Upon the chancel casement, and upon that grave of
mine,
In the early, early morning, the summer sun 'll
shine,
Before the red cock crows from the farm upon the
hill,
When you are warm asleep, mother, and all the
world is still.

---

* A Constellation.

When the flowers come again, mother, beneath the
    waning light,
You'll never see me more in the long gray fields at
    night,
When, from the dry, dark wold, the summer airs
    blow cool
On the oat-grass, and the sword-grass, and the bul-
    rush in the pool.

You'll bury me, my mother, just beneath the haw-
    thorn shade,
And you'll come sometimes and see me, where I am
    lowly laid.
I shall not forget you, mother; I shall hear you when
    you pass
With your feet above my head, in the long and
    pleasant grass.

I have been wild and wayward, but you'll forgive
    me now;
You'll kiss me, my own mother, upon my cheek and
    brow;
Nay, nay, you must not weep, nor let your grief be
    wild;
You should not fret for me, mother: you have another
    child.

If I can, I'll come again, mother, from out my rest-
    ing-place;

Though you'll not see me, mother, I shall look upon
    your face;
Though I cannot speak a word, I shall hearken what
    you say,
And be often, often with you, when you think I'm
    far away.

Good-night, good-night. When I have said good-
    night for evermore,
And you see me carried out from the threshold of the
    door,
Don't let Effie come to see me till my grave be grow-
    ing green :
She'll be a better child to you than ever I have been.

She'll find my garden tools upon the granary floor :
Let her take 'em ; they are hers : I shall never gar-
    den more.
But tell her, when I'm gone, to train the rose-bush
    that I set
About the parlor window, and the box of mignonette.

Good-night, sweet mother : Call me before the day
    is born.
All night I lie awake, but I fall asleep at morn ;
But I would see the sun rise upon the glad New-Year,
So, if you're waking, call me, call me early, mother
    dear !

                            TENNYSON.

The Return of Spring.

BEING A CONCLUSION TO THE FOREGOING PIECE.

I THOUGHT to pass away before, and yet alive I am,
And in the fields all round I hear the bleating of the
    lamb.
How sadly, I remember, rose the morning of the
    year!
To die before the snowdrop came—and now the
    violet's here!

Oh, sweet is the new violet, that comes beneath the
    skies,
And sweeter is the young lamb's voice to me who
    cannot rise;
And sweet is all the land about, and all the flowers
    that blow,
And sweeter far is death than life, to me that long
    to go.

It seemed so hard at first, mother, to leave the blessed
    sun,
And now it seems as hard to stay—and yet His will
    be done!
But still I think it can't be long before I find release,
And that good man, the clergyman, has told me
    words of peace.

Oh, blessings on his kindly voice, and on his silver
hair!
And blessings on his whole life long, until he meet
me there;
Oh, blessings on his kindly heart, and on his silver
head!
A thousand times I blessed him, as he knelt beside
my bed.

He showed me all the mercy, for he taught me all
the sin:
Now, though my lamp was lighted late, there's One
will let me in;
Nor would I now be well, mother, again, if that
could be,
For my desire is but to pass to Him who died for me.

I did not hear the dog howl, mother, or the death-
watch beat;
There came a sweeter token, when the night and
morning meet:
But sit beside my bed, mother, and put your hand in
mine,
And Effie on the other side, and I will tell the sign.

All in the wild March morning, I heard the angels
call;
It was when the moon was setting, and the dark was
over all;

The trees began to whisper, and the wind began to
roll,
And in the wild March morning I heard them call
my soul.

For, lying broad awake, I thought of you and Effie
dear ;
I saw you sitting in the house, and I no longer here.
With all my strength I prayed for both, and so I felt
resigned,
And up the valley came a swell of music on the
wind.

I thought that it was fancy, and I listened in my bed,
And then did something speak to me. I know not
what was said,
For great delight and shuddering took hold of all my
mind,
And up the valley came again the music on the
wind.

But you were sleeping, and I said, It's not for them :
it's mine—
And if it comes three times, I thought, I take it for a
sign ;
And once again it came, and close beside the win-
dow-bars,
Then seemed to go right up to heaven, and die among
the stars.

So now I think my time is near ; I trust it is. I know
The blessed music went that way my soul will have
  to go :
But for myself, indeed, I care not if I go to-day—
But, Effie, you must comfort *her* when I am past
  away.

*   *   *   *   *

Oh, look ! the sun begins to rise, the heavens are in
  a glow ;
He shines upon a hundred fields, and all of them I
  know.
And there I move no longer now, and there his light
  may shine—
Wild flowers in the valley for other hands than mine.

Oh, sweet and strange it seems to me, that, ere this
  day is done,
The voice that now is speaking may be beyond the
  sun,
For ever and for ever, with those just souls and true—
And what is life, that we should moan—why make
  we such ado ?

For ever and for ever, all in a blessed home,
And there to wait a little while, till you and Effie
  come ;
To lie within the light of God, as I lie upon your
  breast—
And the wicked cease from troubling, and the weary
  are at rest.

TENNYSON.

How Peacefully!

How peacefully they rest,
    Cross-folded there
Upon his little breast,
Those tiny hands that ne'er were still before,
    But ever sported with its mother's hair,
Or the bright gem that on her breast she wore!

Her heart no more will beat
    To feel the touch of that soft palm,
That ever seemed a new surprise,
Sending glad thoughts up to her eyes,
    To bless him with their holy calm;
Sweet thoughts, that left her eyes as sweet!

How quiet are the hands
    That wore those pleasant bands!
But that they do not rise and sink
With his calm breathing, I should think
    That he were dropped asleep.
    Alas! too deep—too deep
    Is this his slumber!
    Time scarce can number
The years ere he will wake again—
Oh! may we see his eyelids open then!

He did but float a little way
    Adown the stream of time,
With dreamy eyes watching the ripples play,
    And listening to their fairy chime.

His slender sail
　Ne'er felt the gale ;
He did but float a little way,
　And putting to the shore,
While yet 'twas early day,
Went calmly on his way,
　To dwell with us no more.
No jarring did he feel,
No grating on his vessel's keel.
A strip of silver sand
　Mingled the waters with the land,
Where he was seen no more!
Oh ! stern word—nevermore !

Sonnet

ON THE DEATH OF AN ONLY CHILD.

"It is not the will of my Father which is in heaven that
one of these little ones should perish."

THE day is beautiful, and nature springs
To life and light again.   Where art thou gone
In thy young bloom, my own, my lovely one?
Nor sun, nor balmy air, thy image brings
To bless my longing eyes.   The violet flings
Its rath perfume around ; sweet warblers own
Their joy in varied song ; yet, sad alone,
Can I rejoice, when all surrounding things
Tell of thy opening beauty, shrouded now
In the cold precincts of the silent tomb ?
I did not think to weep thy early doom,
My best beloved !   Yet would I meekly bow
To His decree, who, in the words of love—
" She will not perish !"—whispers from above.

The Child of James Melville,

Born, July 9, 1586. Died about January, 1588.

This page, if thou be a pater [parent, father] that reads it, thou wilt apardone me ; if nocht, suspend thy censure till thou be a father, as said the grave Lacedæmonian, Agesilaus.—*Autobiography of James Melville.*

One time my soul was pierced as with a sword,
  Contending still with men untaught and wild,
When He who to the prophet lent his gourd,
  Gave me the solace of a pleasant child.

A summer gift my precious flower was given ;
  A very summer fragrance was its life ;
Its clear eyes soothed me as the blue of heaven
  When home I turned, a weary man of strife.

With unformed laughter, musically sweet,
  How soon the wakening babe would meet my kiss ;
With outstretched arms its care-wrought father greet :
  Oh ! in the desert what a spring was this !

A few short months it blossomed near my heart ;
  A few short months—else toilsome all and sad ;
But that home solace nerved me for my part,
  And of the babe I was exceeding glad !

Alas! my pretty bud, scarce formed, was dying—
  (The prophet's gourd, it withered in a night!)
And He who gave me all, my heart's pulse trying,
  Took gently home the child of my delight.

Not rudely culled—not suddenly it perished,
  But gradual faded from our love away!
As if still, secret dews, its life that cherished,
  Were drop by drop withheld, and day by day!

My blessed Master saved me from repining,
  So tenderly He sued me for His own;
So beautiful He made my babe's declining,
  Its dying blessed me as its birth had done!

And daily to my board at noon and even
  Our fading flower I bade his mother bring,
That we might commune of our rest in heaven,
  Gazing the while on death without its sting.

And of the ransom for that baby paid,
  So very sweet at times our converse seemed,
That the sure truth of grief a gladness made—
  Our little lamb by God's own Lamb redeemed!

There were two milk-white doves my wife had nour-
    ished;
  And I too loved, erewhile, at times to stand,
Marking how each the other fondly cherished,
  And fed them from my baby's dimpled hand!

So tame they grew, that, to his cradle flying,
 Full oft they cooed him to his noontide rest ;
And to the murmurs of his sleep replying,
 Crept gently in, and nestled in his breast.

'Twas a fair sight—the snow-pale infant sleeping,
 So fondly guardianed by those creatures mild ;
Watch o'er his coséd eyes their bright eyes keeping :
 Wondrous the love betwixt the birds and child !

Still, as he sickened, seemed the doves too dwining,
 Forsook their food, and loathed their pretty play ;
And on the day he died, with sad note pining,
 One gentle bird would not be frayed away.

His mother found it, when she rose sad-hearted,
 At early dawn, with sense of nearing ill ;
And when, at last, the little spirit parted,
 The dove died too, as if of its heart's chill !

The other flew to meet my sad home-riding,
 As with a human sorrow in its coo—
To my dead child and its dead mate then guiding,
 Most pitifully plained, and parted too !

'Twas my first "hansel" * and " propine" † to Heaven :
 And as I laid my darling 'neath the sod—

----

  * Present.   † Earnest, pledge.

Precious His comforts—once an infant given,
And offered with two turtle-doves to God!

MRS. A. STUART MENTEATH.

Casa's Dirge.

VAINLY for us the sunbeams shine;
　Dimmed is our joyous hearth;
O Casa! dearer dust than thine
　Ne'er mixed with mother earth!
Thou wert the corner-stone of love,
　The key-stone of our fate!
Thou art not! Heaven scowls dark above,
　And earth is desolate!

Ocean may move with billows curled,
　And moons may wax and wane,
And fresh flowers blossom; but this world
　Shall claim not thee again.
Closed are the eyes which bade rejoice
　Our hearts, till love ran o'er;
Thy smile is vanished, and thy voice
　Silent for evermore!

Yes, thou art gone, our heart's delight,
　Our boy so fond and dear!
No more thy smiles to glad our sight,
　No more thy songs to cheer;
No more thy presence, like the sun,
　To fill our home with joy!
Like lightning hath thy race been run,
　As swift, as bright, fair boy!

Now winter with its snow departs,
   The green leaves clothe the tree;
But summer smiles not on the hearts
   That bleed and break for thee;
The young May weaves her flowery crown,
   Her boughs in beauty wave;
They only shake their blossoms down
   Upon thy silent grave.

Dear to our souls is every spot
   Where thy small feet have trod;
There, odors breathed from Eden float,
   And sainted is the sod;
The wild bee with its buglet fine,
   The blackbird singing free,
Melt both thy mother's heart and mine—
   They speak to us of thee!

Only in dreams thou comest now
   From Heaven's immortal shore,
A glory round that infant brow
   Which Death's pale signet bore.
'Twas thy fond looks, 'twas thy fond lips,
   That lent our joys their tone;
And life is shadowed in eclipse
   Since thou from earth art gone.

Were thine the fond, endearing ways
   That tenderest feeling prove;

A thousand wiles to win our praise,
   To claim and keep our love.
Fondness for us thrilled all thy veins;
   And, Casa, can it be
That naught of all the past remains
   Except vain tears for thee?

Idly we watch, thy form to trace
   In children on the street;
Vainly in each familiar place
   We list thy pattering feet.
Then sudden o'er these fancies crushed
   Despair's black pinions wave;
We know that sound for ever hushed—
   We look upon thy grave!

O heavenly child of mortal birth!
   Our thoughts of thee arise,
Not as a denizen of earth,
   But inmate of the skies.
To feel that life renewed is thine,
   A soothing balm imparts;
We quaff from out Faith's cup divine,
   And Sabbath fills our hearts.

Thou leanest where the fadeless wands
   Of amaranth bend o'er;
Thy white wings brush the golden sands
   Of Heaven's refulgent shore.

Thy home is where the psalm and song
    Of angels choir abroad,
And blessed spirits all day long
    Bask round the throne of God.

There chance and change are not; the soul
    Quaffs bliss as from a sea,
And years through endless ages roll,
    From sin and sorrow free.
There gush for aye fresh founts of joy,
    New raptures to impart;
Oh! dare we call thee still our boy,
    Who now a seraph art?

A little while, a little while—
    Ah! long it cannot be—
And thou again on us wilt smile
    Where angels smile on thee.
How selfish is the worldly heart,
    How sinful to deplore!
Oh that we were where now thou art,
    Not lost, but gone before!

                      W. D. MOIR.

Armenia.

SHE lies in her coffin,
　Her little sand run !
The golden bowl broken,
　Her happy life done !

No more her sweet prattle
　Will wake us at light ;
No more to each dear one
　She 'll lisp her " Good-night."

How clear used to warble
　Her voice in the song !
What ripe words, yet childish,
　Oft fell from her tongue !

That voice now is silent ;
　We 'll listen in vain,
Amid our sad circle,
　To hear it again !

Oft came a light tapping,
　Scarce touching the floor ;
We knew 't was *her* footstep—
　We 'll know it no more !

We glance at her playthings,
　Her books and her cot,
And tears wet our eyelids,
　For Menie is not !

Hush! Menie still liveth,
    Though not to *our* sight;
Her happy soul basking
    In Heaven's own light.

Her voice still is singing,
    Though not for *our* ear;
She swelleth the chorus
    No mortal may hear.

We ne'er to our bosoms
    Our darling may press,
Yet needs she no token
    Of love's tenderness:

For Jesus hath called her;
    She rests in his arms,
Free now from all sickness,
    Free now from all harms.

She lies in her coffin,
    Life's little sand run;
But, being far nobler,
    She just hath begun!

Oh, would we recall her
    To sin and to pain?
We'll come to *thee*, Menie,
    We'll see thee again!

Our Baby.

WHEN the morning, half in shadow,
Ran along the hill and meadow,
And with milk-white fingers parted
Crimson roses, golden-hearted;
Opening over ruins hoary
Every purple morning-glory,
And out-shaking from the bushes
Singing larks and pleasant thrushes;
That's the time our little baby—
Strayed from Paradise, it may be—
Came, with eyes like heaven above her:
Oh, we could not choose but love her!

Not enough of earth for sinning,
Always gentle, always winning,
Never needing our reproving,
Ever lively, ever loving;
Starry eyes and sunset tresses,
White arms, made for light caresses,
Lips that knew no word of doubting,
Often kissing, never pouting;
Beauty even in completeness,
Over-full of childish sweetness;
That's the way our little baby,
Far too pure for earth, it may be,
Seemed to us, who, while about her,
Deemed we could not do without her.

When the morning, half in shadow,
Ran along the hill and meadow,
And with milk-white fingers parted
Crimson roses, golden-hearted;
Opening over ruins hoary
Every purple morning-glory,
And out-shaking from the bushes
Singing larks and pleasant thrushes;
That's the time our little baby,
Pining here for heaven, it may be,
Turning from our bitter weeping,
Closed her eyes as when in sleeping,
And her white hands on her bosom
Folded like a summer blossom.

Now, the litter she doth lie on,
Strewed with roses, bear to Zion;
Go, as past a pleasant meadow,
Through the valley of the shadow.
Take her softly, holy angels,
Past the ranks of God's evangels;
Past the saints and martyrs holy,
To the Earth-Born, meek and lowly:
We would have our precious blossom
Softly laid in Jesus' bosom.

A Household Lamentation.

Room, Mother Earth, upon thy breast for this young
 child of ours;
Give her a quiet resting-place among thy buds and
 flowers;
Oh! take her gently from our arms unto thy silent
 fold,
For she is calmly beautiful, and scarcely two years
 old,
And ever since she breathed on us hath tender nurs-
 ing known:
No wonder that with aching hearts we leave her
 here alone.

How we shall miss the roguish glee, the merry,
 merry voice,
That in the darkest, dreariest day would make us to
 rejoice!
How sweet was every morning kiss, each parting for
 the night,
Her lisping words, that on us fell as gently as the
 light!
But death came softly to the spot where she was wont
 to rest,
And bade us take her from our home and lay her on
 thy breast.

So, mother, thou hast one child more, and we have
    one child less ;
The sweetest spot in all our hearts seems now a
    wilderness,
From which the warm light of the sun has wandered
    swift and far,
And nothing there of radiance left but Memory's
    solemn star :
We gaze a moment on its light, then sadly turn aside,
As though we now had none to love, and all with her
    had died.

Mother, we know we should rejoice that she has gone
    before—
Gone where the withering hand of death shall never
    touch her more,
Up to the clime of sinless souls, a golden harp to bear,
And join the everlasting song of singing children
    there :
Yet, when we think how dear she was to us in her
    brief stay,
We can but weep that one so sweet so early passed
    away.

                                     R.

And One is Not.

WHEN at eve my children gather
  Round the lowly ingle-side,
Whispering to my spirit, " Father,
  In thy love we each confide ;"
While I press them to my bosom,
  In an overflow of joy,
How I miss that stricken blossom,
  Him who was the only boy !

Often will they talk of brother,
  Even she who knew him not ;
For I think that for another
  He should never be forgot ;
And I love to link their feelings
  With the kindred one away,
Though the thought will oft be stealing,
  That dear form is naught but clay.

Still I bow in bland submission ;
  Even grateful try to be :
One is not ; but, blest condition !
  Providence has left me three.
So I 'll press them to my bosom,
  In an overflow of joy ;
Heaven has gained my cherished blossom,
  God's is now my only boy !

REV. E. C. JONES.

Sonnet.

OFT have I thought they err, who, having lost
That love-gift of our youth, an infant child,
Yield the faint heart to those emotions wild
With which, too oft, strong Memory is crost,
Shrinking with sudden gasp, as if a ghost
Frowned in their path. Not thus the precepts mild
Of Jesus teach; which never yet beguiled
Man with vain promises. God loves us most
When chastening us; and He who conquered
    death
Permits not that we still deem death a curse.
`The font is man's true tomb; the grave his nurse
For heaven, and feeder with immortal breath.
Oh, grieve not for the dead! None pass from earth
Too soon: God then fulfils his purpose in our birth!

SIR AUBREY DE VERE.

The Children at the Golden Gates.

LITTLE travellers Zionward
  Each one entering into rest
In the kingdom of your Lord,
  In the mansions of the blest;
There, to welcome, Jesus waits,
  Gives the crowns his followers win.
Lift your heads, ye golden gates,
  Let the little travellers in!

Who are they whose little feet,
  Pacing life's dark journey through,
Now have reached that heavenly seat
  They had ever-kept in view?
" I from Greenland's frozen land ;"
  " I from India's sultry plain ;"
" I from Afric's barren sand ;"
  " I from islands of the main."

"All our earthly journey past,
  Every tear and pain gone by,
Here together met at last
  At the portals of the sky :
Each the welcome ' COME ' awaits,
  Conquerors over death and sin !"
Lift your heads, ye golden gates,
  Let the little travellers in !

JAS. EDMENSTON

The Good Shepherd.

WHEN on my ear your loss was knelled,
  And tender sympathy upburst,
A little rill from memory swelled,
  Which once had soothed my bitter thirst.

And I was fain to bear to you
  Some portion of its mild relief,
That it might be as healing dew,
  To steal some fever from your grief.

After our child's untroubled breath
  Up to the Father took its way,
And on our home the shade of death,
  Like a long twilight, haunting lay,

And friends came round with us to weep
  Her little spirit's swift remove,
This story of the Alpine sheep
  Was told to us by one we love :

" They in the valley's sheltering care
  Soon crop the meadow's tender prime,
And when the sod grows brown and bare,
  The Shepherd strives to make them climb

" To airy shelves of pasture green,
  That hang along the mountain's side,
Where grass and flowers together lean,
  And down through mists the sunbeams slide ;

" But naught can tempt the timid things
   The steep and rugged path to try,
Though sweet the Shepherd calls and sings,
   And seared below the pastures lie,

" Till in his arms the lambs he takes,
   Along the dizzy verge to go ;
Then, heedless of the rifts and breaks,
   They follow on o'er rock and snow.

"And in those pastures lifted fair,
   More dewy soft than lowland mead,
The Shepherd drops his tender care,
   And sheep and lambs together feed."

This parable, by Nature breathed,
   Blew on me as the south wind free
O'er frozen brooks, that float, unsheathed
   From icy thraldom, to the sea.

A blissful vision through the night
   Would all my happy senses sway,
Of the Good Shepherd on the height,
   Or climbing up the stony way,

Holding our little lamb asleep ;
   And like the burden of the sea
Sounded that voice along the deep,
   Saying, "Arise and follow me."

MARIA LOWELL.

Resignation.

There is no flock, however watched and tended,
　　But one dead lamb is there!
There is no fireside, howsoe'er defended,
　　But has one vacant chair!

The air is full of farewells to the dying,
　　And mournings for the dead;
The heart of Rachel, for her children crying,
　　Will not be comforted!

Let us be patient! These severe afflictions
　　Not from the ground arise,
But oftentimes celestial benedictions
　　Assume this dark disguise.

We see but dimly through the mists and vapors;
　　Amid these earthly damps
What seem to us but sad, funereal tapers
　　May be heaven's distant lamps.

There is no death! What seems so is transition;
　　This life of mortal breath
Is but a suburb of the life elysian,
　　Whose portal we call Death.

She is not dead—the child of our affection—
　　But gone unto that school
Where she no longer needs our poor protection,
　　And Christ himself doth rule.

In that great cloister's stillness and seclusion,
　By guardian angels led,
Safe from temptation, safe from sin's pollution,
　She lives, whom we call dead.

Day after day we think what she is doing
　In those bright realms of air ;
Year after year, her tender steps pursuing,
　Behold her grown more fair.

Thus do we walk with her, and keep unbroken
　The bond which nature gives,
Thinking that our remembrance, though unspoken,
　May reach her where she lives.

Not as a child shall we again behold her ;
　For when, with raptures wild,
In our embraces we again enfold her,
　She will not be a child ;

But a fair maiden in her Father's mansion,
　Clothed with celestial grace ;
And beautiful with all the soul's expansion
　Shall we behold her face.

And though at times impetuous with emotion
　And anguish long suppressed,
The swelling heart heaves moaning like the ocean,
　That cannot be at rest,—

We will be patient, and assuage the feeling
　We may not wholly stay ;
By silence sanctifying, not concealing,
　The grief that must have way.

LONGFELLOW.

Bereavement.

"The Lord gave Job twice as much as he had before."

I MARKED when vernal meads were bright,
 And many a primrose smiled ;
I marked her, blithe as morning light,
 A dimpled three years' child.

A basket on one tender arm
 Contained her precious store
Of spring flowers, in their freshest charm,
 · Told proudly o'er and o'er.

The other wound with earnest hold
 About her blooming guide,
A maid, who scarce twelve years had told :
 So walked they side by side—

One a bright bud, and one may seem
 A sister-flower half blown :
Full joyous on their loving dream
 The sky of April shone.

The summer months swept by : again
 That loving pair I met ;
On russet heath and bowery lane
 Th' autumnal sun had set :

And chill and damp that Sunday eve
 Breathed on the mourner's road.

That bright-eyed little one to leave
   Safe in the saints' abode.

Behind, the guardian sister came,
   Her bright brow dim and pale—
Oh, cheer the maiden!—in His name,
   Who stilled Jairus' wail!

Thou mourn'st to miss the fingers soft
   That held by thine so fast,
The fond-appealing eye, full oft
   Toward thee for refuge cast.

Sweet toils! sweet cares, for ever gone!
   No more from stranger's face
Or startling sound, the timid one
   Shall hide in thy embrace.

Thy first glad earthly task is o'er,
   And dreary seems thy way;
And what if, nearer than before,
   She watch thee even to-day?

What if henceforth by Heaven's decree
   She leave thee not alone,
But in her turn prove guide to thee
   In ways to angels known?

Oh! yield thee to her whisperings sweet:
   Away with thoughts of gloom!

In love the loving spirits greet,
   Who wait to bless her tomb.

In loving hope, with her unseen,
   Walk as in hallowed air;
When foes are strong, and trials keen,
   Think, "What if she be there?"

KEBLE.

The Star and the Child.

A MAIDEN walked at eventide
  Beside a clear and placid stream,
And smiled, as in its depths she saw
  A trembling star's reflected beam.

She smiled until the beam was lost,
  As 'cross the sky a cloud was driven;
And then she sighed, and then forgot
  The star was shining still in heaven.

A MOTHER sat beside life's stream,
  Watching a dying child at dawn,
And smiled, as from its eye she caught
  A hope that it might still live on.

She smiled until the eyelids closed,
  But watched for breath until the even;
And then she wept, and then forgot
  The child was living still in heaven.

R.

Angel Charley.

He came—a beauteous vision—
  Then vanished from my sight,
His cherub wing scarce clearing
  The blackness of my night;
My glad ear caught its rustle,
  Then, sweeping by, he stole
The dew-drop that his coming
  Had cherished in my soul.

Oh! he had been my solace
  When grief my spirit swayed,
And on his fragile being
  Had tender hopes been stayed;
Where thought, where feeling lingered,
  His form was sure to glide,
And in the lone night-watches
  'Twas ever by my side.

He came; but as the blossom
  Its petals closes up,
And hides them from the tempest
  Within its sheltering cup;
So he his spirit gathered
  Back to its frightened breast,
And passed from earth's grim thrall'd
  To be the Saviour's guest.

My boy—ah me! the sweetness,
　The anguish of that word!—
My boy, when in strange night-dreams
　My slumbering soul is stirred;
When music floats around me,
　When soft lips touch my brow,
And whisper gentle greetings,
　Oh tell me, is it thou?

I know by one sweet token
　My Charley is not dead;
One golden clue he left me,
　As on his track he sped:
Were he some gem or blossom,
　But fashioned for to-day,
My love would slowly perish
　With his dissolving clay.

Oh, by this deathless yearning,
　Which is not idly given;
By the delicious nearness
　My spirit feels to heaven;
By dreams that throng my night-sleep,
　By visions of the day,
By whispers when I'm erring,
　By promptings when I pray,

I know this life so cherished,
　Which sprang beneath my heart,

Which formed of my own being
　So beautiful a part;
This precious, winsome creature,
　My unfledged, voiceless dove,
Lifts now a seraph's pinion,
　And warbles lays of love.

Oh, I would not recall thee,
　My glorious angel-boy!
Thou needest not my bosom,
　Rare bird of life and joy!
Here dash I down the tear-drops
　Still gathering in my eyes;
Blest—oh, how blest!—in adding
　A seraph to the skies.

EMILY C. JUDSON.

"Mother, sing Jerusalem."

THE LAST WORDS OF A DYING CHILD.

A child lay in a twilight room,
  With pallid, waxen face;
A little child, whose tide of life
  Had nearly run its race.

Most holy robes the angels brought,
  By holy spirits given,
Ready to wrap the child in them,
  And carry him to heaven.

And shining wings, with clasps of light,
  Two shining wings they bore,
To fasten on the seraph-child,
  Soon as the strife was o'er.

Perchance their beauty made him think
  Of some harmonious word
That often from his mother's lips
  The dying one had heard.

It might be, for he whispered low,
  "Sing, mother, sing," and smiled;
The worn one knelt beside the couch:
  "What shall I sing, my child?"

"Jerusalem, my happy home,"
  The gasping boy replied ;
And sadly sweet the clear notes rang
  Upon the eventide.

"Jerusalem, my happy home,
  Name ever dear to me !
When shall my labors have an end
  In joy, and peace, and thee ?"

And on she sang, while breaking hearts
  Beat slow, unequal time ;
They felt the passing of the soul
  With that triumphal chime.

"Oh, when, thou city of my God,
  Shall I thy courts ascend ?"
They saw the shadows of the grave
  With his sweet beauty blend.

"Why should I shrink at pain or woe,
  Or feel at death dismay ?"
She ceased—the angels bore the child
  To realms of endless day.

Early Lost, Early Saved.

WITHIN her downy cradle there lay a little child,
And a group of hovering angels unseen upon her
  smiled ;
A strife arose among them—a loving, holy strife—
Which should shed the richest blessing over the new-
  born life.

One breathed upon her features, and the babe in
  beauty grew,
With a cheek like morning's blushes, and an eye of
  azure hue ;
Till every one who saw her, were thankful for the
  sight
Of a face so sweet and radiant with ever-fresh
  delight.

Another gave her accents, and a voice as musical
As a spring-bird's joyous carol, or a rippling stream-
  let's fall ;
Till all who heard her laughing, or her words of
  childish grace,
Loved as much to listen to her as to look upon her
  face.

Another brought from heaven a clear and gentle
  mind,
And within the lovely casket the precious gem
  enshrined ;

Till all who knew her wondered that God should be
    so good
As to bless with such a spirit our desert world and
    rude.

Thus did she grow in beauty, in melody, and truth,
The budding of her childhood just opening into
    youth ;
And to our hearts yet dearer every moment than
    before
She became, though we thought fondly heart could
    not love her more.

Then out-spake another angel, nobler, brighter than
    the rest,
As with strong arm, but tender, he caught her to his
    breast :
" Ye have made her all too lovely for a child of mor-
    tal race,
But no shade of human sorrow shall darken o'er her
    face.

" Ye have tuned to gladness only the accents of her
    tongue,
And no wail of human anguish shall from her lips
    be wrung ;
Nor shall the soul that shineth so purely from within
Her form of earth-born frailty, ever know the taint
    of sin.

"Lulled in my faithful bosom, I will bear her far
    away,
Where there is no sin nor anguish, nor sorrow, nor
    decay;
And mine a boon more glorious than all your gifts
    shall be—
Lo! I crown her happy spirit with immortality!"

Then on his heart our darling yielded up her gentle
    breath,
For the stronger, brighter angel, who loved her best,
    was DEATH!

BETHUNE.

The Eternal Gain.

Oh! think that while you 're weeping here,
  His hand a golden harp is stringing ;
And, with a voice serene and clear,
His ransomed soul, without a tear,
  His Saviour's praise is singing.

And think that all his pains are fled,
  His toils and sorrows closed for ever ;
While He whose blood for man was shed
Has placed upon his infant head
  A crown that fadeth never !

And think that in that awful day
  When darkness sun and moon is shading
The form that midst its kindred clay
Your trembling hands prepared to lay,
  Shall rise to life unfading !

Then weep no more for him who 's gone
  Where sin and suffering ne'er shall enter ;
But on that great High Priest alone,
Who can for guilt like ours atone,
  Your whole affections centre.

Dr. Huie.

Epitaph in the Churchyard of Berne.

SWEET babe, from griefs and dangers
    Rest here for ever free;
We leave thy dust with strangers,
    But oh, we leave not *thee!*

Thy mortal sweetness, smitten
    To scourge our souls from sin,
Is on our memory written,
    And treasured deep therein;

While that which is immortal
    Fond Hope doth still retain,
And saith, "At heaven's bright portal
    Ye all shall meet again."

                J. MOULTRIE.

A Death-Bed.

Her suffering ended with the day,
　　Yet lived she at its close,
And breathed the long, long night away
　　In statue-like repose.

But when the sun, in all his state,
　　Illumed the eastern skies,
She passed through Glory's Morning-gate,
　　And walked in Paradise!

James Aldrich.

Another.

We watched her breathing through the night,
　　Her breathing soft and low,
As in her heart the wave of life
　　Kept heaving to and fro.

So silently we seemed to speak,
　　So slowly moved about,
As we had lent her half our powers
　　To eke her being out.

Our very hopes belied our fears,
　　Our fears our hopes belied;

We thought her dying when she slept,
And sleeping when she died.

For when the morn came, dim and sad,
And chill with early showers,
Her quiet eyelids closed—she had
Another morn than ours.

THOMAS HOOD.

A Ministering Angel.

MOTHER, has the dove that nestled
  Lovingly upon thy breast
Folded up his little pinion,
  And in darkness gone to rest?

Nay, the grave is dark and dreary,
  But the loved one is not there;
Hear'st thou not its gentle whisper
  Floating on the ambient air?

It is near thee, gentle mother,
  Near thee at the evening hour;
Its soft kiss is in the zephyr,
  It looks up from every flower.

And when, night's dark shadows fleeing,
  Low thou bendest thee in prayer,
And thy heart feels nearest heaven,
  Then thy angel babe is there!

EMILY JUDSON.

Cease to Weep.

MOTHER, o'er thy daughter bending,
On her bed of death attending,
Cease to heave those sighs heart-rending—
 Cease to weep.

Vain the tears you now are weeping,
Vain the watch you now are keeping:
Calmly now in peace she's sleeping
 Death's long sleep.

For her now the Son is pleading
To that Father ne'er unheeding;
And her spirit, homeward speeding,
 May not stay.

Mourn not, then, that she is leaving
Early thus a world deceiving,
Where so many oft are grieving
 Death's delay.

J. H. GRANVILLE.

Our Eldest=Born.

Thou bright and star-like spirit,
  That in my visions wild
I see mid heaven's seraphic host,
  Oh, canst thou be my child !

My grief is quenched in wonder,
  And pride arrests my sighs ;
A branch of this unworthy stock
  Now blossoms in the skies !

Our hopes of thee were lofty ;
  But have we cause to grieve ?
Oh, could our proudest, fondest wish
  A nobler fate conceive ?

The little weeper—tearless ;
  The sinner—snatched from sin ;
The babe—to more than manhood grown
  Ere childhood did begin.

And I, thy earthly teacher,
  Would blush thy powers to see :
Thou art to me a parent now,
  And I a child to thee.

Thy brain, so uninstructed
  While in this lowly state,
Now threads the mazy tracks of spheres,
  Or reads the book of fate.

Thine eyes, so curbed in vision,
  Now range the realms of space,
Look down upon the rolling stars,
  Look up—in God's own face.

Thy little hand so helpless,
  That scarce its toys could hold,
Now clasps its mate in holy prayer,
  Or strikes a harp of gold.

Thy feeble feet, unsteady,
  That tottered as they trod,
With angels walk the heavenly paths,
  Or stand before their God.

Nor is thy tongue less skilful
  Before the throne divine ;
'T is pleading for a mother's weal,
  As once she prayed for thine.

What bliss is born of sorrow !
  'T is never sent in vain :
The heavenly Surgeon maims to save ;
  He gives no useless pain.

Our God, to call us homeward,
  His only Son sent down,
And now, still more to tempt our hearts,
  Has taken up our own.

THOMAS WARD.

God Looked Among his Cherub Band.

God looked among his cherub band,
　And one was wanting there,
To swell along the holy land
　The hymns of praise and prayer.

One little soul which long had been
　Half way 'tween earth and sky,
Untempted in a world of sin,
　He watched with loving eye.

It was too promising a flower
　To bloom upon this earth,
And God did give it angel power,
　And bright celestial birth.

The world was all too bleak and cold
　To yield it quiet rest ;
God brought it to his shepherd-fold,
　And laid it on his breast.

There, mother, in thy Saviour's arms,
　For ever undefiled,
Amid the little cherub band,
　Is thy beloved child.

We are Seven.

——— A simple child,
That lightly draws its breath,
And feels its life in every limb,
What should it know of death?

I MET a little cottage Girl;
She was eight years old, she said;
Her hair was thick with many a curl
That clustered round her head.

She had a rustic, woodland air,
And she was wildly clad;
Her eyes were fair, and very fair:
Her beauty made me glad.

" Sisters and brothers, little Maid,
How many may you be?"
" How many? Seven in all," she said,
And wondering looked at me.

"And where are they? I pray you tell."
She answered, " Seven are we:
And two of us at Conway dwell,
And two are gone to sea.

" Two of us in the churchyard lie——
My sister and my brother;
And in the churchyard cottage, I
Dwell near them with my mother."

"You say that two at Conway dwell,
  And two are gone to sea;   .
Yet ye are seven! I pray you tell,
  Sweet Maid, how this may be."

Then did the little Maid reply:
  "Seven boys and girls are we;
Two of us in the churchyard lie,
  Beneath the churchyard tree."

"You run about, my little Maid,
  Your limbs they are alive;
If two are in the churchyard laid,
  Then ye are only five."

"Their graves are green, they may be seen,"
  The little Maid replied,
"Twelve steps or more from my mother's door,
  And they are side by side.

"My stockings there I often knit,
  My kerchief there I hem;
And there upon the ground I sit—
  I sit and sing to them.

"And often after sunset, sir,
  When it is light and fair,
I take my little porringer,
  And eat my supper there.

" The first that died was little Jane :
    In bed she moaning lay,
Till God released her of her pain,
    And then she went away.

" So in the churchyard she was laid ;
    And when the grass was dry,
Together round her grave we played,
    My brother John and I.

"And when the ground was white with snow,
    And I could run and slide,
My brother John was forced to go,
    And he lies by her side."

" How many are you, then," said I,
    " If they two are in heaven ?"
The little Maiden did reply,
    " Oh, Master, we are seven !"

" But they are dead : those two are dead !
    Their spirits are in heaven !"
'T was throwing words away ; for still
    The little Maid would have her will,
    And said, " Nay, we are seven !"

WORDSWORTH.

The Safety of the Infant Dead.

They only can be said to possess a child for ever, who
have lost one in infancy.

Our beauteous child we laid amidst the silence of
the dead ;
We heaped the earth, and spread the turf above the
cherub-head ;
We turned again to sunny life, to other ties as dear,
And the world has thought us comforted, when we
have dried the tear.

And time has rolled its onward tide, and in its ample
range
Has poured along the happiest paths vicissitude and
change ;
The flexile forms of infancy their earliest leaves have
shed,
And the tall, stately forest trees are waving in their
stead.

We guide not now our children's steps, as we were
wont before,
For they have sprung to manhood, they lean on us
no more ;
We gaze upon the lofty brow, and time and thought
have cast
A shade, through which we seek in vain the memory
of the past.

And do we mourn the other change, which mocks
    our memory here?
Ah no! 't is but the answered wish of many a secret
    prayer:
Centre of all our fondest hopes, we live but in their
    fame,
But our love, as to a little child, how can it be the
    same?

We still have one—and only one—secure in sacred
    trust;
It is the lone and lovely one that's sleeping in the
    dust.
We fold it in our arms again, we see it by our side
In the helplessness of innocence, which sin has never
    tried.

All earthly trust, all mortal years, however light
    they fly,
But darken on the glowing cheek, and dim the
    eagle eye;
But there, our bright, unwithering flower—our spirit's
    hoarded store—
We keep through every chance and change, the same
    for evermore.

The Spirit's Song of Consolation.*

DEAR parents, grieve no more for me ;
   My parents, grieve no more ;
Believe that I am happier far
   Than even with you before.
I've left a world where woe and sin
   Swell onwards as a river,
And gained a world where I shall rest
   In peace and joy for ever.

Our Father bade me come to him,
   He gently bade me come ;
And he has made his heavenly house
   My dwelling-place and home.
On that best day of all the seven
   Which saw the Saviour rise,
I heard the voice you could not hear,
   Which called me to the skies.

I saw, too, what you could not see—
   Two beauteous angels stand ;
They smiling stood, and looked at me,
   And beckoned with their hand ;
They said they were my sisters dear,
   And they were sent to bear

---

* Supposed to be addressed by the departed spirit of a
boy to his parents, who, had lost two other children before
him.

My spirit to their blessed abode,
　To live for ever there.

Then think not of the mournful time
　When I resigned my breath,
Nor of the place where I was laid,
　The gloomy house of death;
But think of that high world, where I
　No more shall suffer pain,
And of the time when all of us
　In heaven shall meet again.

F. W. P. GREENWOOD.

Epitaph on a Child.

Sleep on, my babe! thy little bed
　Is cold, indeed, and narrow;
Yet calmly there shall rest thy head,
And neither mortal pain nor dread
　Shall e'er thy feelings harrow!

Thou may'st no more return to me;
　But there's a time, my dearest,
When I shall lay me down by thee,
And when of all, my babe shall be,
　That sleep around, the nearest!

And sound our sleep shall be, my child,
　Were earth's foundations shaken;
Till He, the pure, the undefiled,
Who once, like thee, an infant smiled,
　The dead to life awaken!

Then if to Him, with faith sincere,
　My babe at death was given,
The kindred tie that bound us here,
Though rent apart with many a tear,
　Shall be renewed in heaven.

R. Huie.

The Master's Call.

" Rise," said the Master, "come unto the feast."
  She heard the call, and came with willing feet;
  But thinking it not otherwise than meet,
  For such a bidding, to put on her best,
  She is gone from us for a few short hours
  Into her bridal-closet, there to wait
  For the unfolding of the palace-gate,
  That gives her entrance to the blissful bowers.
  We have not seen her yet, though we have been
  Full often to her chamber-door, and oft
  Have listened underneath the postern green,
  And laid fresh flowers, and whispered short and
      soft ;
  But she hath made no answer, and the day
  From the clear west is fading fast away.

H. Alford.

Entering In.

THE valleys of Paradise echo again,
  And harp-notes of heaven are melting away;
Glad voices of melody catch the soft strain,
  An angel, an angel shall join us to-day!

She enters and pauses, her little bare feet
  Rest shining and white on the glittering ground;
Her ruby lips quiver, as fearing to meet
  The bright infant cherubs that gather around.

They pass their soft hands o'er her luminous brow,
  With angelic winning her spirit beguile;
They whisper the language which cherubims know,
  Her blue eyes grow liquid with heaven's first
    smile.

"Wings, wings for the angel!" Behold! she is
    plumed.
  Bring harps, golden harps for the beautiful one;
Her brow with a glorious wreath is illumed,
  Her reign of eternity sweetly begun.

The Winning Shepherd

To win his flocks to fields above,
  Where dewy grass lies clothed in green,
The goodly shepherd takes with love
  The gentle lambs his arms between;

While on his breast they trusting lie,
  He climbs aloft to verdure rare;
Then finds he's won them toward the sky—
  The mother-fold all gathering there!

So Christ, in love, to win his folds,
  And lift the parent's heart to heaven,
Their precious babes his bosom holds—
  He only takes what he has given—

And bears them through the pearly gates,
  And keeps for us our jewels there;
For well he knows the heart but waits
  To follow where its treasures are.

                                        D.

For Charlie's Sake

C. D. P.—*Ob.* Oct. 28, 1861.

THE night is late, the house is still;
The angels of the hour fulfil
Their tender ministries, and move
From couch to couch, in cares of love.
They drop into thy dreams, sweet wife,
The happiest smile of Charlie's life,
And lay on baby's lips a kiss,
Fresh from his angel-brother's bliss ;
And, as they pass, they seem to make
A strange, dim hymn, "For Charlie's sake."

My listening heart takes up the strain,
And gives it to the night again,
Fitted with words of lowly praise,
And patience learned of mournful days,
And memories of the dead child's ways.

His will be done, His will be done!
Who gave and took away my son,
In "the far land" to shine and sing
Before the Beautiful, the King,*
Who every day doth Christmas make,
All starred and belled for Charlie's sake.

For Charlie's sake I will arise ;
I will anoint me where he lies,
And change my raiment, and go in
To the Lord's house, and leave my sin

* Isaiah 33 : 17.

Without, and seat me at his board,
Eat, and be glad, and praise the Lord.
For wherefore should I fast and weep,
And sullen moods of mourning keep?
I cannot bring him back, nor he,
For any calling, come to me.*
The bond the angel Death did sign,
God sealed—for Charlie's sake and mine.

I'm very poor—his slender stone
Marks all the narrow field I own;
Yet, patient husbandman, I till
With faith and prayers, that precious hill,
Sow it with penitential pains,
And, hopeful, wait the latter rains;
Content, if, after all, the spot
Yield barely one forget-me-not—
Whether or figs or thistles make
My crop, content for Charlie's sake.

I have no houses, builded well—
Only that little lonesome cell,
Where never romping playmates come,
Nor bashful sweethearts, cunning-dumb—
An April burst of girls and boys,
Their rainbowed cloud of glooms and joys,
Born with their songs, gone with their toys;
Nor ever is its stillness stirred
By purr of cat, or chirp of bird,
Or mother's twilight legend, told
Of Homer's pie, or Tiddler's gold,

* 2 Samuel 13 : 16, 23.

Or fairy, hobbling to the door,
Red-cloaked and weird, bannèd and poor,
To bless the good child's gracious eyes,
The good child's wistful charities,
And crippled changeling's hunch to make
Dance on his crutch, for good child's sake.

How is it with the child? 'Tis well;
Nor would I any miracle
Might stir my sleeper's tranquil trance,
Or plague his painless countenance;
I would not any seer might place
His staff on my immortal's face,
Or, lip to lip, and eye to eye,
Charm back his pale mortality.
No, Shunammite! I would not break
God's stillness. Let them weep who wake.*

For Charlie's sake my lot is blest;
No comfort like his mother's breast,
No praise like hers; no charm expressed
In fairest forms hath half her zest.
For Charlie's sake this bird's caressed
That Death left lonely in the nest;
For Charlie's sake my heart is dressed,
As for its birth-day in its best;
For Charlie's sake we leave the rest
To Him who gave, and who did take,
And saved us twice, for Charlie's sake.

* * *.

* 2 Kings 4 : 26, 29, 34.

Our Baby.

OF all the darling children
　　· That e'er a household blessed
We place our baby for compare
　　With the fairest and the best;
She came when last the violets
　　Dropped from the hand of Spring;
When on the trees the blossoms hung—
Those cups of odorous incense swung,
　　When dainty robins sing.

How glowed the early morning
　　After a night of rain,
When she possessed our waiting hearts
　　To go not out again;
"Dear Lord," we said, with thankful speech,
　　"Grant we may love thee more,
For this new blessing in a cup
　　That was so full before!"

September, 1858.

This year, before the violets
　　Had heralded the spring,
And not a leaf was on the trees
　　Nor robin here to sing,
An angel came one solemn night,
　　Heaven's glory to bestow,
And take our darling from our sight—
What could we, Lord, at morning light,
　　But weep, and let her go!

How dark the day that followed
 That dreary night of pain,
Those eyes now closed, and never more
 ·To open here again !
"Dear Lord," we said, with broken speech,
 "Grant we may love thee more,
For this new jewel in the crown
 Where we had *two* before !"

·   A. D. F. R.

September, 1860.

Baby looking out for me.

Two little busy hands patting on the window,
  Two laughing, bright eyes looking out at me ;
Two rosy-red cheeks dented with a dimple ;
  Mother-bird is coming ; baby, do you see ?

Down by the lilac-bush, something white and azure,
  Saw I in the window as I passed the tree ;
Well I knew the apron and shoulder-knots of ribbon ;
  All belonged to baby, looking out for me.

> Talking low and tenderly
>   To myself, as mothers will,
> Spake I softly : " God in heaven,
>   Keep my darling free from ill,
> Worldly gain and worldly honors
>   Ask I not for her from Thee ;
> But from want and sin and sorrow,
>   Keep her ever pure and free."

Two little waxen hands,
  Folded soft and silently ;
Two little curtained eyes,
  Looking out no more for me ;
Two little snowy cheeks,
  Dimple-dented nevermore ;
Two little trodden shoes,
  That will never touch the floor ;
Shoulder-ribbon softly twisted,
  Apron folded, clean and white ;
These are left me—and these only
  Of the childish presence bright.

Thus He sent an answer to my earnest praying,
   Thus He keeps my darling free from earthly stain,
Thus He folds the pet lamb safe from earthly straying;
   But I miss her *sadly* by the window-pane,
Till I look above it: then, with purer vision,
   Sad, I weep no longer the lilac-bush to pass,
For I see her, angel-pure and white and sinless,
   Walking with the harpers, by the sea of glass.

       Two little snowy wings
         Softly flutter to and fro,
       Two tiny childish hands
         Beckon still to me below;
       Two tender angel eyes
         Watch me ever earnestly
       Through the loop-holes of the stars;
         Baby's looking out for me.

My Darling's Shoes.

God bless the little feet that can never go astray,
For the little shoes are empty, in the closet laid away!
Sometimes I take one in my hand, forgetting, till I see
It is a little half-worn shoe, not large enough for me;
And all at once I feel a sense of bitter loss and pain,
As sharp as when, two years ago, it cut my heart in
      twain.

O little feet that wearied not! I wait for them no more,
For I am drifting on the tide, but *they* have reached
      the shore;
And while the blinding tear-drops wet these little
      shoes so old,
She stands unsandled in the streets that pearly gates
      enfold;
And so I lay them down again, but always turn to
      say:
God bless the little feet that *now so surely* cannot
      stray.

And while I thus am standing, I almost seem to see
Two little forms beside me, just as they used to be;
Two little faces lifted, with their sweet and tender
      eyes.
Ah me! I might have known that look was born of
      Paradise.
I reach my arms out fondly, but they clasp the empty
      air!
There's nothing of my darlings but the shoes they
      used to wear.

Oh! the bitterness of parting cannot be done away,
Till I see my darlings walking where their feet can
    never stray;
When I no more am drifted upon the surging tide,
But *with them safely* landed upon the river-side;
Be patient, heart! while waiting to see *their* shining
    way,
For the little feet in the golden street can never go
    astray.

Only a Year.

One year ago, a ringing voice,
  A clear blue eye,
And clustering curls of sunny hair,
  Too fair to die.

Only a year, no voice, no smile,
  No glance of eye,
No clustering curls of golden hair,
  Fair but to die!

One year ago, what loves, what schemes
  Far into life!
What joyous hopes, what high resolves,
  What generous strife!

The silent picture on the wall,
  The burial-stone,
Of all that beauty, life, and joy,
  Remain alone!

One year, one year, one little year,
  And so much gone!
And yet the even flow of life
  Moves calmly on.

The grave grows green, the flowers bloom fair,
  Above that head;
No sorrowing tint of leaf or spray
  Says he is dead.

No pause or hush of merry birds,
    That sing above,
Tells us how coldly sleeps below
    The form we love.

Where hast thou been this year, beloved ?
    What hast thou seen ?
What rising fair, what glorious life,
    Where thou hast been ?

The veil ! the veil ! so thin, so strong !
    'Twixt us and thee ;
The mystic veil ! when shall it fall,
    That we may see ?

Not dead, not sleeping, not even gone ;
    But present still,
And waiting for the coming hour
    Of God's sweet will.

Lord of the living and the dead,
    Our Saviour dear !
We lay in silence at thy feet
    This sad, sad year !   MRS. STOWE.

Fairy Tales.*

THE picture of a little child
　　That comes to us from o'er the sea,
Why hath it thus my heart beguiled,
　　Why such a charm for me?

Before it oft I stop and gaze,
　　And pass the rarer pictures by,
Until the shopman, in amaze,
　　Would seem to ask me why.

He does not know, nor need I tell,
　　Where, in that face, a look I see
Of one who for a while did dwell
　　On earth to comfort me.

The picture of a little child,
　　A book, a child, and nothing more;
And she to quiet reconciled
　　By FAIRY TALES of yore.

What joy, what wonder on her face,
　　And such as children only know;
And Art has caught each changeful grace,
　　And will not let it go.

O childish face! thou art not mute,
　　Thou giv'st my thought mysterious range;
Here in thy presence I compute
　　A story sweet and strange:

* A picture by a foreign artist of a little child seated, and reading a large book.

The story of a little life,
  So brief, and yet withal so sweet;
'Twould seem a dream, but for the strife
  That made the life complete.

Thus many a time in days gone by,
  A child, who dwells with us no more,
(How deep the shadows now that lie
  Where sunlight was before,)

Would sit, a book within her hand,
  Her eye intent upon the page,
As though she well did understand
  What did her sight engage.

O blessed child! I see thee still!
  My heart o'erleaps the solemn years,
And eyes thou once with light didst fill,
  Thou fillest now with tears.

And yet through Sorrow's cloud and mist
  My eager sight is swift to run
Through sapphire hues, and amethyst,
  And glory of the sun;

Until thy face, with wondrous change,
  I, as in vision, clearly see;
O child of mine! O marvel strange!
  What might I learn of thee!

Two score of years, what have they brought
  Of knowledge to compare with thine?
The narrow reach of human thought,
  To that which is divine!

The mysteries of our mortal state,
  At which I shrink as they unfold,
Nor fear nor wonder can create
  In them who God behold!

Sweet child, not mine as heretofore,
  Still mine in glory yet to be;
Dear Lord, could I desire more
  Concerning her of thee!

O throbbing heart! thy longings cease;
  Come, patient Lord, thy grace bestow,
And turn this sorrow into peace,
  That shall more perfect grow.

This picture of a little child,
  By one who dwells across the sea,
Thus hath it oft my heart beguiled,
  And been a joy to me!   A. D. F. R.

www.ingramcontent.com/pod-product-compliance
Lightning Source LLC
Chambersburg PA
CBHW030612040726
47497CB00008B/2940